THE PANDORA DEVICE

CAMP HAWTHORNE BOOK ONE

Joyce McPherson

Also by Joyce McPherson

Books in the Camp Hawthorne series

The Revere Factor

The Dickens Connection

THE PANDORA DEVICE

DEVICE

CAMP HAWTHORNE BOOK ONE

Joyce McPherson

Cover design by C.T. McPherson

Published by Candleford Press

ISBN: 1533240043
ISBN-13: 978-1533240040

To Garth, who makes every day an adventure.

CHAPTER ONE

Grandma didn't like to talk about my parents, even when I asked. The sparkle would fade from her eyes, and her arms would wrap around me and hold me tight.

She seemed to gather strength from the bags of clothing, newspapers and odd gadgets she brought home every day, sorting them into piles at night until the rooms were crammed full with only a path down the middle.

For me, the rooms were like caves filled with treasure, and I used to invite Lindsey over to help me explore. I liked to think about the things we found—a black typewriter, a bomber hat, a spindly lace umbrella—they all belonged to someone once. There must be stories.

But the stories just stayed in my head until the day we found the box.

We were sorting through a pile of clothes, and Lindsey had tied a fringed shawl around her head so that only wisps of her blond hair showed.

"Look Stella. I'm a gypsy queen," she said, rattling some bangles on her arms.

"And I'm a pirate." I buckled on a leather belt and poked through another mound of stuff in hopes of finding boots.

Near the bottom, a moldy boot was caught under a rickety sewing machine. I tugged at it, but it wouldn't budge. I finally pulled so hard that the machine creaked, and a rusty box flew free with the boot.

"Treasure," Lindsey said.

I rubbed the grime from the lid, and a sudden lump rose in my throat. Faint letters were scratched on the box—Franny. My mother's name.

My fingers prickled as I opened the lid.

Inside lay some faded photos and a red bandana, tied in a knot. I loosened it, and a key chain fell out. For a moment it sparkled in the dim room, but I looked again and it was just blue and white plastic, braided into a rope with an empty key ring at the end.

"Did you see that?" Lindsey asked, touching the key ring lightly.

"Let's show Grandma," I said.

We dashed down the hall to her library and squeezed through the stacks of newspapers that filled the room like yellowed skyscrapers.

She sat in her recliner in the midst of them, and I had a quick image of those towers slowly tilting until they whooshed across the floor and through the front door. That was my biggest nightmare—that the whole neighborhood would find out about Grandma's collections.

"Look what we found," I said.

Her face crinkled in a smile at the sight of us, but when she saw the box she put a hand on her heart. "I thought that was lost. It's your mother's keepsakes from camp." She pulled out one of the pictures. "And here she is with your father." Her gray eyes swept the room with the sad look she got when she talked about the past.

I held my breath as I took the photo. A girl with a bandana gripped one end of an oar painted with the words *Camp Hawthorne*. By her side a boy grabbed the other end and waved at the camera. The picture gave me a heavy feeling in my chest. When I was little I didn't think about my parents much, but now that I was in sixth grade, it was different.

"Something odd about that camp," she said softly.

I hugged the box, hoping she'd tell us more. "What was it?"

She hesitated, and her hands fell weak in her lap. "I can't remember, Stella." I touched her arm, but she was far away, lost in her thoughts.

I pulled Lindsey aside. "Let's see if we can find the camp on the White Whale."

The White Whale was our name for my old-style laptop, clunky and thick. It came from one of Grandma's friends and was so ancient, it barely connected to the internet. The case was shiny white except for one corner where scratch marks covered a logo. I'd hidden the damage with a round sticker, and Lindsey had painted *Stella* on it.

We ran down the street to Lindsey's house to use her wi-fi. Peanut butter and granola cookies were cooling on a wire rack, and we filled a plate while we waited for the screen to flicker to life.

The White Whale chugged as I nibbled on a warm cookie. "Wouldn't it be exciting if the camp was still there?"

Lindsey studied the photo. "Look what's written on the back—Franny and Dan. Their names almost rhyme. How romantic."

That's what I like about Lindsey. She appreciates details like that.

The White Whale beeped, and I typed in the words *Camp Hawthorne.* A link zipped into view.

"It still exists." My voice seemed to come from somewhere far away.

I tapped the mouse, and a picture appeared of a lake with three green canoes lined up on the shore. In the distance, pine trees ringed the lake under a blue sky. I stared at the image, trying to memorize every detail. Had my parents paddled those canoes once?

"There's a tab for admissions," Lindsey said, her voice squeaking.

I clicked the tab, and the lake slipped away, replaced by a white screen. I read aloud:

Dear Educators,
Camp Hawthorne is a private camp for students who pass a specialized screening test. If you have

4

students with an interest in camp, please contact us at the email address below.

"What does that mean?" Lindsey asked.

"I don't know," I said. "But I'm going to find out." My brain felt fizzy like a bottle of root beer. I'd found a link to my parents at last.

If anyone could find out more about Camp Hawthorne, it would be Mrs. Taylor, our school guidance counselor. I met her when I started having trouble breathing. It was like a big fat cat was sitting on my chest. My teacher noticed I was taking deep breaths and sent me to the school nurse, who said nothing was wrong and sent me on to Mrs. Taylor. I had to visit her once a month and report on my breathing. It didn't get any better, but I enjoyed talking to her. Her office was filled with posters of kids doing interesting things, like building robots and hiking in the woods. She always asked a lot of questions and then told me to stop worrying about things. Easy for her to say.

The next day I got to school early and tried to duck into Mrs. Taylor's office before anyone noticed. Unfortunately, Ellen and her gaggle of friends spotted me. "You're not in trouble again, are you?" she asked, straightening the headband in her curly red hair. There was an incident years ago with my grandmother, and Ellen never let me forget it.

I plastered a smile on my face. "No, just doing a little research." I hoped my tone sounded nonchalant.

Nonchalant was one of our vocabulary words this week, and it meant *calm*. I was determined to be more nonchalant.

Mrs. Taylor was pecking at her keyboard with two fingers but seemed glad to take a break when she saw me in the doorway. "What can I do for you, Stella?"

I sat in the plump chair she had for students. "Have you ever heard of Camp Hawthorne?" I asked.

"Should I know about it?" She adjusted her glasses and peered at the posters on her walls as though they might have an answer.

"It's a summer camp," I said. "They have information online, but you have to take a test."

"Hmm, that may be a good sign. Entrance exams often come with scholarships." She typed the camp name and clicked through the pages online. "The information's here. We don't have much time before summer break, but let me see what I can find."

Ellen and her gang were waiting for me when I came out of Mrs. Taylor's office.

"Did you get your *research* done?" Ellen asked. She turned to her friends and spoke in a loud voice so that everyone in the hallway would hear. "Stella had to see the guidance counselor, but she doesn't want us to know."

The other girls giggled, and my face burned. I stuck my chin in the air. "If you must know, I was researching options for camp."

Ellen opened her mouth to reply, but I walked away before she cooked up something else to say.

For the rest of the morning I swung between hope that Mrs. Taylor would contact Camp Hawthorne and doubt that she could do anything. I knew she meant well, but it wasn't reasonable to expect her to drop everything and investigate camp for me.

At lunch only two chairs were left, so Lindsey and I had to sit next to Jayden. He had brown skin and close cropped hair, and with the camouflage shirts he always wore, he looked more like a soldier than a kid. He lived across the street from me, and we did everything together when we were little. But now he walked around, never answering, as though he was under interrogation in an enemy prison. He shifted away from us and bent over his book.

Lindsey held up a necklace made from feathers and beads. "It's called a dream catcher."

When I first met Lindsey four years ago, she was wearing a white tutu and a crown. Now that we were in sixth grade, she dressed almost normally, but I still had to be ready for whatever wild idea she might have.

She dangled the dream catcher in the air, and the feathers whirled around. "Magic's coming," she said.

"You don't still believe in magic?" Sometimes I had to remind Lindsey of the real world.

"What's wrong with it?" She slipped the necklace over her head and looked at me expectantly.

That was a tough one. I still liked books about magic, but I was planning to be a scientist when I grew up. "Well, it's not scientific."

"What if magic is just super-advanced science?" She pulled out a pen and began doodling swirls on her lunch bag. "You know our teacher said there's stuff even scientists don't know yet."

She had a point. People from the Middle Ages would probably assume we had magic if they saw us talking on the phone or flying in an airplane.

I was still thinking about Lindsey's ideas when Mrs. Taylor, nodding and smiling, caught me in the hallway after lunch. "It's the strangest thing about that camp—I'd never heard of it, but it has the endorsement of the school superintendent *and* the PTA. The camp will provide scholarships if we have a qualifying team of three students, so I've arranged for our school to host the test."

"What if they can't find enough kids who want to take the test?"

"Not a problem at all," she said as she scuttled back to her office. "They're giving it to your entire class."

I walked in late to class to hear our teacher giving the announcement for the exam. Everyone groaned, and some of them looked at me accusingly. I wondered how word had gotten out so fast. Probably Ellen. That meant none of the other girls would want to go, even if they passed the test. I took a deep breath. The heavy-cat-on-my-chest feeling was coming back.

≈✠≈

CHAPTER TWO

≈✠≈

On the way home from school, I found Jayden in front of his house, slamming a basketball through the rickety hoop. I called his name, and he scowled, pausing to spin the ball on one finger. "What do you want?"

"I was wondering if you'd go to camp if you passed the screening test," I said.

He dribbled the ball around his driveway, his arms a blur. The ball pounded like gun shots, and he sprang for a basket. "No."

"Mrs. Taylor said we have to get three qualifying students for a team."

I asked him again, but he shook his head. It made me mad when Jayden wouldn't answer, but it didn't do any good to argue. It was easier talking to his grandmother. Miss Charlotte lived with his family, and she was the whirlwind of the neighborhood. She took charge of the neighborhood watch and the community clean-up and everything else she could organize. I had an idea that if I told her about camp, she'd make Jayden go.

Jayden shot one basket after the other, but I wouldn't give him the satisfaction of sticking around while he ignored me. I marched back to my yard, trying to keep from exploding.

Our house was the last on the row and suffered from a general sagging. The roof slanted at crazy angles, and the gingerbread trim was barely recognizable because of bits that had rotted away. Grandma's pushcart was parked behind the porch. She must have come home early from her thrift store rounds. Sure enough, broken baskets and bags full of stuff were piled near the door.

I was holding my breath, and I let it out in a sigh.

Tackling the larger bags first, I carried soft items like clothes to the piles in the living room. Newspapers I took to the library, where I found Grandma asleep in her recliner.

I was hoping to tell her the news about Camp Hawthorne, but it could wait till dinner. Instead, I sat on the porch and got out my math homework. Today it was percents and probabilities, which intrigued me. Numbers are usually dependable, but they can lie, too. For example, you can have a 90% chance of sunshine and still get rain. That's because there's a 10% chance you *won't* get sunshine. You have to keep an eye on that possibility.

Jayden passed by, hunched over an armload of books as though they were secret files. Maybe they were. He made trips like this to the library every week, but whenever I asked him what the books were about, he just shrugged.

I hoped to see his grandmother soon. I figured my chances were pretty close to 100%. She stopped by every day to mention something that needed to be cleaned up, and my grandmother pretended she was not at home.

Grandma was not at home for other people too. Like the brown people. We called them that because of their clothes. Even the women wore them—brown raincoats with clunky square-toed brown shoes to match. Lindsey and I made up sinister plots about them, but her mother said they were probably just employees of the water company. I wasn't convinced, and it worried me that we were seeing more of them lately. According to my calculations, there was a 50% chance of seeing one on any particular day.

As for Miss Charlotte, my prediction proved true before I even got to problem twenty-five in my math book. She came striding toward our house, walking tall with her shoulders back. The neighbors said she carried the weight of the world on her shoulders, but she didn't look it.

"I want to discuss these piles on your porch," she began as a way of greeting.

I looked around in a panic—I'd missed four garbage bags in the corner. "These belong inside," I said, grabbing two bags and dragging them toward the door.

Miss Charlotte nodded her approval. "Jayden tells me Mrs. Taylor has arranged a test for summer camp."

I hefted the bags through the door and went for the other two. "Do you think Jayden will come?"

"Honey, he can say otherwise, but if he gets into that camp, I'll make sure he's there."

My arms felt powerful enough to carry four bags at once. "Thank you, Miss Charlotte. I was worried we wouldn't get enough kids to go."

Her eyes narrowed. "Oh, you'll get enough. I'll make sure of it."

I watched her make her way to Lindsey's house, where I knew her parents would learn about the summer camp idea. With Miss Charlotte on my side, things were going to happen.

I went back inside, and Grandma stirred at the sound of my steps. "Dinner time already?" She shifted forward in the chair, her shoulders pulled low.

"Don't worry about dinner," I said quickly. "I'll make something for tonight."

I found a can of tuna in the bin for mystery cans. Tuna cans were easy to identify because they were thinner than the rest. The tall cans were usually vegetables—corn or green beans or beets. When the labels fell off, the store sold them for almost nothing. Grandma and I made a game of guessing what was in them, and I'd found that if I shook them gently I could pick the right vegetable. Grandma thought it was a nifty trick.

As we ate our tuna sandwiches, I told Grandma my news. "Do you remember the photos from Camp Hawthorne?" I asked. "Lindsey and I found out it's still there, and they're going to take a team of three kids from our school."

Grandma's forehead puckered, and I hoped I hadn't upset her.

"I don't have to go if you need me here."

"Nonsense. I've been taking care of you since you were a baby." Her face relaxed. "Did you see what I found at the thrift store today? Two jackets and a whole bag of socks."

I'd stopped telling her I had enough clothes a long time ago. She would just remind me how fast children grew, and how it was her responsibility to take care of me now that my parents were gone. I didn't want to have that discussion again.

After dinner I sat by the front window to read until bedtime. When it grew too dark to see the words on the page, I stared out at the glowing street lamps and the moths flickering around the globes. I was thinking about camp and how to convince Jayden to go when a man in a brown raincoat stepped from behind a tree. He looked up at our roof and then stooped to pick up something from the ground.

I caught my breath and leaned back into the curtains. But the dust made me sneeze, and when I looked again the man was gone.

The day of the test finally came, and our teacher got us ready after lunch. She made a big deal about us being the first class at our school to take the exam. "It will not be like a math or English test," she said. "This camp is for students with special abilities, and it's quite an honor to receive an invitation. All expenses are paid."

A short knock sounded on the door, and a man with a green bow tie, blue shirt, khakis and black high top sneakers walked into the room. I'd never seen a grown-up dressed that way before.

The man's gaze swept back and forth across the rows of desks. "My name is Mr. Parker, and I'm from Camp Hawthorne."

"What's it like?" Ellen asked. She wasn't interested in camp before, but now she wanted to know everything about it.

Instead of an answer, Mr. Parker began passing out blue test booklets. "Please print your name on the cover," he said.

I wrote on the line, making my letters straight and precise. I imagined Lindsey would be doodling a flower above the "i" in her name.

"Now open to the first page."

I read the instructions and then relaxed. We were given a story, and we simply had to tell what happened next. I wrote as fast as I could, ideas popping into my mind. If this was all there was to the test, it might be fun. But I was only on my second page when Mr. Parker asked us to stop and turn to the next section, which was filled with puzzles. Some of them were like the ones I did with Grandma in the newspaper, but most of them were strange, involving rotating shapes in your head and matching them to other shapes.

"Huh," Jayden muttered from behind me, but I heard his pencil scratching on the paper. His grandmother must have talked to him.

After the paper test, Mr. Parker took us in groups of four and held up cards with symbols on them. Then he turned them over, and we took turns guessing what was on the cards. I had no idea what we were doing, but I played along. Ellen was in my group, and she made a great fuss about touching each card before she made her guess.

"What a stupid test," she muttered so only I would hear.

My stomach was churning like the time I did too many somersaults in gym class. The second part of the exam was too hard. What if I didn't pass the test? In my mind, I saw the three green canoes on the lake. My parents sat in one of them as it floated farther and farther from the shore.

CHAPTER THREE

The next week Mrs. Taylor asked me to come to her office after school. Lindsey and Jayden were already there when I arrived. Mrs. Taylor was simmering about something. She kept pushing her glasses up the bridge of her nose while glancing out the window at the paved parking lot.

"I asked you three to come to my office because I have something important to tell you." She paused and looked out the window again. Nothing had changed, so she continued, her voice rising with excitement. "A team from our school is receiving a scholarship to Camp Hawthorne, and Mr. Parker is coming to present the invitations."

At that moment Mr. Parker sauntered into the office. Mrs. Taylor beamed. "Here he is now."

Mr. Parker wore the same outfit with the black high tops and green bow tie. He went to each of us in turn and shook our hands, and he even remembered our names. Then he brought out three envelopes. Lindsey squeaked when he handed the first one to her.

Before he presented my invitation, he held it up for a moment. "Expect the unexpected, Stella," he said solemnly. I took the crisp envelope in my hand. I was so happy I thought I would stop breathing altogether. We had a team, and we were going to camp!

But there was a problem. Jayden wouldn't accept his invitation. He left Mr. Parker standing there, holding it out to him.

"I've changed my mind," he mumbled and slunk out of the room.

I dashed after him, arguing the whole way to the playground. "We need a team if we're going to get the scholarship," I said. "It's not fair to the rest of us."

He turned away, dribbling the basketball around the court.

Mr. Parker had followed right behind us, and he caught the ball on a rebound. The corners of his mouth curved up in a lopsided smile, and he twirled the ball around on his finger.

Jayden raised an eyebrow but kept the frown.

"Why not read the invitation, at the very least?" Mr. Parker suggested. He squinted at the basket and took a shot. It bounced off the rim, and Jayden caught the ball in one smooth motion, sending it back through the hoop.

"Maybe," he replied.

"Cheerio, then." Mr. Parker slipped the invitation into Jayden's shirt pocket. The motion was so quick that Jayden didn't know it was happening until too late. He pulled out the envelope and stared at it.

"I'm telling Miss Charlotte you got your invitation today," I crowed and ran back to our neighborhood as fast as I could so he wouldn't have a chance to deny it.

At home I climbed the stairs to my room, which Grandma called the "robin's nest." I liked it because it was so high in the house that the bags of Grandma's findings didn't filter up there. One wall had an old bookcase that Lindsey's mom had helped me paint pale blue. The White Whale sat on the top shelf with my favorite books lined up beside it. My bed was tucked under the sloping roof, and Lindsey and I had made a mobile of paper birds to swirl above it.

I sat on the edge of the bed and studied the invitation— a tan envelope with a square containing the letter C and H pressed onto it. I ran my fingers over the ridges, admiring how fancy it was, before slipping my finger under the flap and loosening the glue so the envelope didn't tear. The invitation was made of the same tan paper and appeared to be written by hand with a fountain pen. It crackled when I unfolded it. I read:

An invitation is extended to Miss Stella Harski
to attend Camp Hawthorne for two weeks.
A scholarship is provided, but each camper
is responsible to bring sheets, towels, a sleeping bag,
clothing, swimsuit and other necessities.
No cell phones or other electronic devices please.
The bus will depart at 9 a.m.
from Williams Middle School on June 21st.

I raced downstairs to show Grandma, who was puttering around in the kitchen. She was as giddy as I was over the invitation.

"We have to begin packing right away," she said. She led the way to the living room and pushed through the piles, wheezing a little as she stirred up dust.

"Wait Grandma, let me do that for you." I squeezed in behind her. "Just tell me what you're looking for."

She stopped to consider. "I know there's a suitcase in here somewhere and at least one sleeping bag."

I scanned the room. It seemed like the sleeping bag ought to be in the corner. As I waded through the mounds of stuff, a moldy suitcase banged me on the knees, and I pulled it out triumphantly.

"Good girl," Grandma said. "And there should be some bug spray in here, too."

By dinnertime we had a heap at the foot of the stairs with hiking boots, two baseball caps, a rusty can of bug spray, a butterfly net and a sleeping bag.

Grandma gave the butterfly net a swish. "I always thought this would be useful."

"I bet I'll be the only camper with all the necessities," I said.

Even though camp was a week away, I packed everything that night. Before closing the suitcase, I added the things from my mother's box: the red bandana, the key chain, and the camp photo of my parents, which I put in a plastic frame.

⟪⟫

The last day of school was Field Day, which Lindsey loved, but I thought pointless. School had run out before we had time for the baking soda experiment in the science book, but the teachers thought it was okay to use the last day for games?

Jayden was always the class star on Field Day. He ran the fastest and threw the ball the straightest, and it got on my nerves how the other kids who ignored him all year started clapping him on the back and cheering for him.

Ellen stood next to me while we waited for the egg relay. "I heard you have to go to that camp," she said.

"No one has to go," I said. "It just so happens I've never been to camp and particularly wanted to go this year."

"Is Jayden going?" she asked, and the way she said it made me feel like she was accusing me of something. "I heard you arguing with him about it."

Lindsey was just returning with the egg, so I had a chance to escape. I held out my spoon and took off down the field. I didn't want to admit to Ellen that even on the last day of school I didn't know if Jayden was coming.

School let out early, and I got home in time to meet the mailman. "A letter for you, Stella," he said, giving me a wink. "Perhaps a secret admirer."

That was our private joke, but it was true that the letter came without a return address. Just a flimsy white envelope with my name and address on the outside. I pulled out a piece of paper printed with the words:

STELLA, FOR YOUR OWN SAFETY, DON'T TRY TO FIND OUT ABOUT YOUR PARENTS.

My hand trembled, and the words seemed to blur. I stood in the front hall trying to breathe slowly like Mrs. Taylor taught me and wondering if I should show Grandma. She knew about Camp Hawthorne and my parents, but who else knew? What if it was the brown people? My stomach clenched, and I pushed that thought away. The brown people were just a story that Lindsey and I made up.

I breathed in and out again. Camp Hawthorne was my only link to my parents. I couldn't let anything get in the way of going there. I crumpled the paper and threw it in the trash. My chest ached as though I'd just run the hundred yard dash, but I told myself I'd think about the message later. I was going to camp tomorrow.

%%%

CHAPTER FOUR

%%%

I woke up the next morning with a jittery stomach. I'd had a nightmare that there were only two people waiting for the bus, and the driver shook his head and said, "Sorry, I can't take you if you don't have a team of three."

I ate a hurried breakfast of cornflakes and took Grandma her breakfast in bed. I was anxious about leaving her by herself.

She snorted at the sight of coffee and cereal arranged on a tray. "I'm just in danger of being lonely. I haven't lost the use of my legs."

"Are you sure you'll be all right?"

"Of course I will." She drew me close in a hug. "Go have fun at camp."

Before I left, I opened the suitcase and made sure my parents' photograph was still on top. I tied my mother's bandana around my neck and put her key chain in my pocket. Then I let myself out the front door, closing it quietly behind me. I felt as though any sound might disturb the morning stillness that hung over the neighborhood. I breathed in the smell of wet grass and summer roses. Vacation had really and truly begun.

I walked to Lindsey's house, and her little sister Peggy opened the door. "Mom's making Lindsey wake up," she said. "Want to see my wiggly tooth?"

I admired her tooth while Lindsey called from upstairs that she was almost ready. She ran down the steps, her blonde hair in a long braid down her back. I wished I'd thought of something special to do with my hair for camp. Braids would probably look better with my mousy brown hair.

Lindsey must have read my face. "Don't worry, Stella. You look fine. Doesn't she, Mom?"

Lindsey's mother was an artist, and I trusted her. She studied me for a moment. "You don't want to cover those gray eyes," she murmured, reaching out to brush my hair back from my face. "Now you look just right for an adventure."

I hoped it was true.

We gathered our bags, and Lindsey's mother drove us to school.

"Nice," Lindsey said, tapping the butterfly net. "Where'd you get it?"

"Grandma found it."

"She can find anything," she said, running her fingers though the silky net.

I thought of Grandma alone in our sagging old house and hoped she would be all right.

At the school Lindsey's mother waited with us. She looked up at the sky, which had dimmed to gray. "I'm afraid it looks like rain on your first day of camp."

But I was worrying about other things. "What if we don't have a team of three—will they let us on the bus?"

"You worry too much," Lindsey said.

She was always telling me that—like the time I found the chart that showed the risk of dying from a car crash. It was only 1%, but both my parents had died that way. If a probability of 1% could happen, other bad things could happen. Like death by accidental injury—that was 3%. I took a deep breath and held it until I felt better.

Unfortunately, it didn't last long. The message from yesterday still weighed on my mind. "Do you suppose there's anything wrong with trying to learn more about my parents?"

Lindsey shrugged. "Why would there be?" She paused and looked at me. "Why are you asking?"

I wasn't sure I was ready to tell her about the warning note. "It's just that Grandma won't talk about them. I wondered if there might be some secret."

She laughed. "That's even more reason to find out about them."

At that moment my watch beeped for the hour— 9:00—and I spotted Jayden in the distance. His ball cap was pulled low over his eyes, and he was carrying his bag and a basketball. He slouched to a stop a few feet away as though he didn't want to admit we were waiting for the same bus.

I wanted to smile at him, but I was afraid it would make him leave.

I picked up my suitcase, ready for the bus which would be coming any minute. But instead of the bus, a sleek red car purred up in front of the school, and Ellen stepped out. She had a rolling suitcase with a matching navy sleeping bag strapped to the top.

I clutched the butterfly net a little tighter. "What are you doing here?" I asked.

"I'm going to camp, too." She straightened the headband in her curly red hair and arranged her luggage on the curb. Then she stiffly hugged her mother through the car window.

"Are you sure you don't want me to wait with you?" her mother asked.

"Mom, we already talked about this," she said.

Her mother's face fell, but she tooted the horn cheerfully and pulled off.

Ellen was inspecting everyone's baggage, and she pointed to Lindsey's pillowcase with the purple ponies. "You *are* a rising seventh grader, right?"

"Of course," she replied, giving Ellen one of her level stares.

I moved in front of my suitcase and tried to hide the butterfly net behind my back.

Lindsey's mom came to the rescue. "I'm glad to see you, Ellen. I didn't know you were going to camp."

Ellen smirked. "My father contacted the camp and made special arrangements for me to go."

"But you told everyone camp was a stupid idea," I said.

She tossed her curls behind her shoulder. "I changed my mind."

I looked at Lindsey out of the corner of my eye. She was humming and staring off into space. Jayden turned away, spinning his ball on one finger. I wanted to ask more questions, but before I could figure out what to say, a white bus rounded the corner and stopped in front of the school with a puff of blue smoke.

On the side was the square logo with the C and H like our invitations. The driver opened the door, and I held my breath. Would he let us all on the bus?

Mr. Parker appeared in the doorway, clipboard in hand. He wore the same black high top sneakers and bow tie, but today he'd added bright green suspenders. "Jayden, Stella, Lindsey and Ellen," he called out. I let out my breath in a whoosh.

Mr. Parker opened a door in the side of the bus, and we stowed our bags with a collection of boxes, suitcases and odd shapes that might have been instrument cases.

Lindsey's mother hugged both of us. "Don't forget to write home," she called as we went up the steps.

The bus was already crowded with kids, crammed three to a seat. Some of them wore Camp Hawthorne T-shirts, and I figured they had been to camp before. The only empty seats were near the back. I sat between Lindsey and Ellen, while Ellen looked around the bus, as though trying to find someone else to talk to.

Lindsey squirmed next to me. "This is so exciting," she whispered.

Jayden found an empty seat directly in front of us, next to a tall girl with long black hair. He leaned his arms on his basketball and looked at his shoes.

The door banged shut, and the bus lurched forward.

Mr. Parker stood swaying against the pole in the front. "I must ask everyone to stay in their seats for this next passage." he said.

The word "passage" sounded odd to me.

The bus rolled around the back of the school and turned onto Perkins Lane which used to be a railway track. We bumped along the road where the track was paved over.

"Why are we going this way?" I muttered to Lindsey. "There's nothing out here but the train tunnel."

Simmons Hill loomed ahead of us. The tunnel was cut in the rock with tangles of vines covering the hole like a green curtain.

Ellen pinched my arm. "We're not going through the tunnel, are we?" she said.

"We can't. There are bars across the entrance. We'll have to turn off a side road."

But the bus didn't turn. It sped straight ahead so fast that it wasn't until we plunged through the mouth of the tunnel that I realized the bars were gone.

CHAPTER FIVE

Ellen shrieked and the bus hurtled into blackness. I gripped the seat in front of me and tried to breathe. If the possibility of dying by car accident was 1%, what was the possibility of dying in a bus speeding through a pitch black tunnel?

Kids were shouting and hurrahing like they were on a roller coaster. "The last tunnel's the best!" someone whooped.

The darkness pressed in, and my eyes strained for any hint of light. Only the rocking of my seat assured me we were still moving. Then the bus veered around a curve, and I was thrown against Lindsey. When I regained my balance, I saw a glimmer of blue in the distance—a circle of sky that rapidly grew larger and larger, until we shot out into the yellow light of a summer day.

A hush fell over the bus, as though everyone was waiting for something. Outside the windows, every sign of our neighborhood had disappeared. Even the old railroad track was gone. Instead, in every direction were green fields with cows grazing here and there.

"Where are we?" I said.

The girl sitting next to Jayden tossed her head, and her long black hair flicked across my face. "Newbies," she muttered.

"What does that mean?" I whispered to Lindsey.

She was back in her dream world staring at the sky. "Puffy clouds," she murmured. She was right—the sky had changed. It was no longer the same overcast sky from our wait in front of the school.

A minute later the bus turned onto a dirt road. A wooden Camp Hawthorne sign hung from an arch made from three logs. The other kids erupted in cheers. "We're here," hooted someone. Things were happening so fast that I felt dizzy.

Mr. Parker sprang to his feet. "Welcome to camp," he said, beaming at us.

Some of the other campers looked as confused as I felt. They peered ahead through the windows and then back the way we came.

Ellen dug an elbow in my ribs. "I never would've come if I'd known it was just on the other side of Simmons Hill," she said.

Lindsey was gazing dreamily out the window. "Is it Simmons Hill?" she asked.

Ellen squinted at her, and for a moment I saw a flicker of uncertainty. "Ridiculous," she said.

But I wasn't so sure. Maybe Lindsey was right. Could it be super-advanced science—some kind of mass hypnosis or a new kind of transportation?

The bus rumbled its way into the woods, and the chatter on the bus intensified. Mr. Parker waved his arms, and the entire bus exploded into a song that resembled donkeys braying. I caught the words "Camp Hawthorne" and "dear old camp," but they were all mixed together.

The bus veered around a corner and rolled up a driveway toward the most bizarre house I'd ever seen. It was at least three stories tall with windows topped by pointed roofs and chimneys that curved out like one of Grandma's vases. Black and orange bricks made diamond patterns in the red walls, and a round room with glass windows and a cone-shaped roof bulged out from one side. The glass room appeared to be filled with leafy trees. The middle section was a tall tower, and around it, like a skirt, frilled the roof of a porch that ran along the front and side.

Everyone stampeded off the bus, and Mr. Parker gathered the new campers on the porch, where dozens of three-legged stools clustered around barrels topped with checker boards. A guy and a girl, who might have been college-age, left their game and came over to us.

The guy wore a safari hat and khaki shirt with a blue bandana. "This is Buckeye," Mr. Parker said. "He's head counselor for the boys." He turned to the girl. "And this is Skeeter—head counselor for the girls. They're going to take you from here."

Skeeter waved. She had two pencils stuck through the twist of brown hair on top of her head.

"Art pencils," Lindsey murmured next to me. "Cerulean blue and indigo."

"This is Twain House, one of the dormitories," Buckeye began, speaking over the muttering of the crowd. He had a funny accent—maybe English or Australian. "And everyone will eat their meals over there." He pointed to another brick building that was not as fancy as the main house.

Ellen sniffed. "Looks like a garage."

Buckeye read names from the clipboard, and six campers followed him through the door. Skeeter motioned to the rest of us. "Your dorms are farther off, so everyone else come with me." I glanced back and saw Jayden slouching near the end, behind a group of three boys wearing red T-shirts.

I carried my suitcase in one hand and tucked my sleeping bag under the other arm as we hiked down the driveway and onto a dirt track. Skeeter slowed up to let Lindsey and me walk alongside her. After our crazy ride, it felt good to breathe the tangy air, which smelled of pine needles.

"I like your pencils," Lindsey said.

Skeeter slipped the blue one out of her hair. "It's believed that owls are the only animals that can see the color blue," she said. "And the Aztecs believed this color to be protective, so they used the turquoise stone in their shields."

Lindsey was fingering one of her braids, a faraway look in her eye. I was sure she was planning to wear pencils in her hair to school next year.

The trail twisted around, and Skeeter called a halt at a huge stone in the path, where some older kids waited. She patted the stone. "Campers, this is the Junction Stone. Get your bearings on this marker, and you'll never get lost. Five paths meet here, one from each dorm. Your counselors are going to take you from here."

Calling names from a list, she assigned us to the waiting counselors. The red shirts and a boy in overalls joined the team from our school. Our counselor was Eugene, and he wore all black with a spiky haircut. He scowled and led us to the left path, which ran along a shallow creek.

The day was growing warmer, and mosquitoes buzzed around my head. My suitcase banged against my legs and the butterfly net kept getting tangled with my sleeping bag. I watched Ellen rolling her bag on its wheels and thought how nice it must be to have an up-to-date suitcase.

We rounded a cluster of pine trees and someone said "ooh." The house stood under an ancient tree, and the shadows wavering on the gray siding seemed to dissolve the building into the woods. Bits of roof ran in every direction with chimneys poking out at strange angles. The windows reflected back the light like blind eyes.

"Who would want to stay here?" Ellen whispered in my ear. "It's creepy." I ignored her, stepping closer to Eugene to hear what he was saying.

"This is Hawthorne House," he announced in a monotone voice. "And this tree is called the Hawthorne Elm."

Lindsey gazed up into the branches. "Lovely tree."

Eugene grunted and turned abruptly to step into the house. "The camp store is here." He seemed determined to deliver information with the least number of words possible.

The store had a narrow counter standing in front of rows of granola bars, T-shirts and brightly colored plastic cord on reels—the same stuff used for my mother's key chain. I slipped my hand in my pocket to make sure it was still there.

We followed him through a door and up a narrow set of steps to a landing on the second floor. "Girls, go that way," he said with a flick of his head, then turned and led the boys up the next flight of stairs.

The gloom of the hallway was depressing, but I pushed open the first door I came to and found a long, low room with sunny windows along one wall. A girl was spreading sheets on a bed, and she jumped back and held the door for us. "Hi y'all. I was expecting you any minute." She had blue eyes and a matching blue shirt that said *Perform Random Acts of Shakespeare*.

"I like your shirt," I said.

"Are you into Shakespeare?"

The only Shakespeare play I'd ever seen was an old movie Grandma brought home called *The Taming of the Shrew*. "I guess," I said. "I don't really know much about him."

"I'll have to get you hooked," she said. She stuck out her hand. "I'm Cecily, your CIT."

I shook her hand, feeling oddly grown-up. "What's a CIT?"

"Counselor-in-training." Her words rattled off her tongue like beads on a plate. "Let me know if you need anything. I'm on kitchen duty, so I've got to scoot or the cook will be in a tizzy. When you get unpacked, come back up to Twain House."

Before I could ask any questions, she was gone.

Our dormitory was certainly an improvement on the other parts of the house. The room smelled of lemon floor cleaner, and pots of geraniums hung from hooks at the corners. Along both sides stood three sets of bunk beds.

"How many people sleep in one room?" Ellen asked.

This was the kind of math question I enjoyed. "Twelve," I said.

Ellen stuck her nose in the air. "Every camp I've ever been to had only four to a room."

Lindsey sat down with a bounce on one of the cots. "Twelve is more fun—we'll meet lots of new people."

Ellen scowled and put her bags on the cot under Cecily's bunk. The other beds were already claimed, so Lindsey and I got the remaining bunk at the far end.

"Can I take the top?" she asked, swinging herself up the metal frame. She knelt on the mattress, her head almost brushing the underside of the sloping roof. "This is going to be great!"

Another girl breezed in while we were unrolling our sleeping bags. She was the girl with the long black hair who sat in front of us on the bus. She unzipped her bag, and Lindsey's eyes widened at the pile of colorful shirts and designer jeans she stuffed in the plastic bins by her bed.

The girl smoothed her hair and came over to us. "What's that?" she asked, pointing at the butterfly net I'd draped by my cot. Before I could answer, she snickered. "No one uses those anymore. It's barbaric to catch butterflies. We use these babies in the twenty-first century." She lifted the camera she carried around her neck and clicked a picture of me staring at her with my mouth open.

Another girl peered around the doorway. "Joanne, where have you been? Everyone's looking for you."

The girl ambled after her without giving us another glance.

"I guess her name is Joanne," Lindsey said in a small voice. "I hope we brought the right kind of stuff."

I thought of my grandmother and her delight as she helped me pack, and I shoved my suitcase under the cot. "She may have a nice camera, but she doesn't know everything," I said. "We can unpack later. Let's go find Jayden."

CHAPTER SIX

Ellen came with us, and for once she was actually pleasant. She must have felt as odd as we did in this new place. We found Jayden in the camp store, drinking a purple liquid from a paper cup. "It's called bug juice," he said, a slight blush of purple staining the corners of his lips. "But it doesn't have bugs in it. Weird camp."

We followed the path back to Twain House and arrived just as the gong sounded for lunch. I wasn't prepared for the crowd that streamed into the dining hall. There must have been at least four bus loads of kids. I was standing still, trying to figure out where to go, when someone pushed me from behind. I turned and saw Joanne, the girl from our dorm.

"Sorry," she said in an exaggerated way so I would know she didn't mean it.

"What's with her?" Lindsey asked.

I was wondering the same thing, but I didn't know what to do. Fortunately Cecily ushered us to a table. The boys with red shirts were already sitting there. "We're the boys from Bromley," said one of them. He had curly brown hair and so many freckles that they spilled over onto his arms.

Jayden muttered to the rest of us, "Private boys' school near DC."

The freckled boy continued, "My friends call me Freddy, and this is Garrett and Coop."

The other boys didn't seem interested in talking.

We told them our names, and Garrett wrote them in a tiny notebook he kept in his pocket. "Field notes," Freddy explained.

Joanne and her friends sat at the next table. I must have been frowning at her, because Cecily laughed. "You look like the dog that caught the car. Did you meet Joanne already?"

"She came in when we were unpacking."

"Don't let her bother you. She treats everyone that way. Now who wants to be the runner today?"

It turned out, every table had a runner. They got the pitchers of bug juice and platters of food to bring from the kitchen. To my surprise, Ellen volunteered.

Since all of us were first-time campers, Cecily kept up a commentary on how the meals worked. If anyone wanted seconds, the runner would take our platter back for more. The food that wasn't eaten had to be scraped into a can in the middle of the table. "It's for the pigs," she said.

"There are pigs at camp?" I asked.

"Sure, who else is going to eat all the slops y'all leave behind? Actually, the pigs belong to Aunt Winnie. She has a little place near the lake. Now, who wants to volunteer for dishwashing?"

I was curious about everything at camp, so my hand shot up. Jayden volunteered, too. I gathered the plates from our table, and Jayden collected the pile from Joanne's group. No one had volunteered there. "It happens sometimes," Cecily said with a disapproving look at the neighboring table.

Jayden was halfway to the kitchen when it happened. He didn't see a bench that had been pushed into the aisle, and he stumbled against it. His plates flew in the air, and it looked like he would go sprawling across the bench, but the next moment he caught his balance and stretched forward to catch the plates. One by one they rattled back into a pile, and the silverware clattered on top of them. Not a single thing fell to the floor. The nearby campers began to clap, and Jayden ducked into the kitchen before the rest of the room broke into applause.

I followed him through the swinging doors. "That was amazing!"

He scowled.

I didn't get Jayden. One minute he was volunteering to help, and the next he was clamming up when you said something nice.

The cook was a giant man with scars on his face and arms, where his sleeves were rolled up. He stared at us, then jerked his thumb toward the door. "Out back."

Behind the dining hall we found about twenty bins, some with suds and some with clear water, lined up against the wall.

I was trying to figure out what to do next when Cecily appeared. "Jayden, you must've gone a minute in thirty seconds back there," she said. "Have you considered going professional with that trick?"

He didn't say anything, but his frown relaxed.

She had her own stack of plates, which she dumped in a bin of soapy water. "You should've seen Mr. Parker's face when you caught all those plates. I thought he was going to shout *Halleluiah*."

"Why?" I asked. I couldn't imagine a pile of plates was that important.

"Never you mind for now. Let's get these dishes scrubbed." Cecily showed us how to wash the plates in soapy water, then rinse them in clear water, before stacking them in the empty dish pans.

We started scrubbing our dishes, and other campers joined us. I was finishing my plates when one of the volunteers cried out, "I've found a pearl!"

Cecily motioned to us. "Feel in the bottom of your bins and see if you have any."

I ran my hand through the soapy water, and there were two pearls. Jayden found one, too. "You take them to the cook, and he'll give you a candy bar," she said.

"Weird camp," Jayden said, but he was smiling as we stood in line with the others to get our chocolate.

Mr. Parker was waiting when we got back to our table. "Jayden and I need to talk."

The guarded look returned to Jayden's face, and I watched them walk out, a prickle of worry starting up again.

"Why so glum?" Cecily asked. "You have a free hour after lunch—you should go exploring."

"Shouldn't we wait for Jayden?"

"Mr. Parker won't be done with him for at least an hour," she said.

What did that mean?

I started toward the door, but a display on the far side of the room caught my eye. Rows of canoe paddles, painted with names, covered the wall. "Cecily, what are those?"

She shrugged. "It's a Camp Hawthorne tradition. The names of the head counselors are recorded on a paddle. Buckeye and Skeeter will be featured this year."

I walked closer and scanned the names. Near the top of one column hung a paddle painted with "Franny and Dan." My heart leapfrogged into my throat. I reached as high as I could to touch the edge of the handle, and my fingers tingled.

Lindsey was right behind me. "You found them," she whispered.

Ellen called from the doorway. "Are you coming or not?"

The image of my parents holding the paddle flashed in my mind. Perhaps I could find more clues about them. "Come on," I said. "Let's explore."

Cecily showed us the path to the lake but had to get back to kitchen duty. We joined the boys from Bromley, who were pulling compasses and tiny notebooks from their pockets. Freddy wore something that looked like a medallion around his neck. He turned it over to show us a tiny screen on the other side. "It's a GPS receiver," he said. "Our whole team got the invitation after we won the Mid-Atlantic Geo-caching Contest."

"How does it work?" asked Lindsey.

Freddy pushed a button. "Those are your coordinates."

"Like latitude and longitude?" Lindsey locked onto the device like it was one of her dream catchers.

"Precisely."

"Where are we now?" I asked

He read off some numbers that meant nothing to me.

"Doesn't it tell you the name of the place?"

"No, you have to use a map for that."

"We know where we are, anyway," Ellen said, giving me one of her pathetic looks. "We're just past the tunnel in Simmons Hill."

But I wasn't so sure about that.

The path to the lake meandered behind Twain House and down a slope covered with trees. Roots grew across the trail, so you had to watch your feet, and Lindsey looked like she was dancing as she skipped over them.

Freddy and his gang kept stopping to take readings, which they copied into their notebooks.

"When will we get to the lake?" I asked after the fifth stop for readings.

Freddy grinned, and his freckles spread over his face in dozens of new constellations. "We have no idea, but we can tell our location from satellite."

"Ha," Ellen said. "Any fool would know it's over there." She pointed through the trees, where I could make out the sparkle of sun on water.

"Let's run," I said.

"Wait," Freddy called. "You're not supposed to run on trails like this."

I dashed, anyway. The trail curved around again, and I caught my breath at the sight of the lake, rippling in a slight breeze. Three canoes lay on the shore, like the picture online. Even the pine trees looked the same, and the sky was just as blue. I pulled off my shoes and waded into the lake. The first shock of cold sent a thrill to my brain: my parents were here once.

Ellen splashed into the lake beside me, a huge smile taking hold of her cheeks, like she couldn't help it. "Good job finding this camp."

I almost fell over into the water. It was the first nice thing she'd ever said to me. We waded along the shore picking up pebbles from the shallows, and before I knew it, Freddy was calling that our time was up.

I sighed and dried my hands on my jeans. This was just the beginning of finding clues to my parents. I couldn't wait to get started on all the camp stuff.

≈୨≈

CHAPTER SEVEN

≈୨≈

Back at the dining hall, Skeeter rounded up the new campers for a game. Jayden was back, but he didn't tell us anything. He kept shaking his head like my grandmother does when she can't find something.

"Why did Mr. Parker want you?" I asked.

"He's going to explain after the game," he said.

After that I couldn't concentrate on the game. It was supposed to help us learn everyone's name. We got in a circle and went around saying our name and something we would bring to camp that started with the same letter. ("It doesn't have to be something you really brought," Skeeter said.) Then we repeated the names and items of everyone who went before. Fortunately I was next to the boys from Bromley, and I already knew them. Freddy brought a frying pan, Garrett brought a GPS (no surprise) and Coop brought a chicken, which I thought was clever of him.

My turn came too fast. "I'm Stella, and I brought ...string," It was the only thing I could come up with at the last minute.

After the game, Buckeye got out his guitar. A bunch of older kids, including Eugene and Cecily, stood beside him. "The counselors-in-training are going to help you learn our camp song," Buckeye said with enthusiasm. Eugene stared straight ahead as though the last thing he wanted to do was sing in front of a bunch of first year campers, but Buckeye strummed his guitar and the CITs launched into the song we'd heard on the bus. It actually sounded better with only a few people singing. The words were easy—just "Camp Hawthorne, dear old camp" sung over and over. We joined in, and we sounded pretty good. I glanced over at Jayden, and he was singing—I had to know what Mr. Parker told him.

Mr. Parker stood in the back during the song but came forward now. "Gather round everyone. Time for a history lesson." We sat on the floor while he stood in front of the wide fireplace with its mantle shelf of books. They had bindings in blue, green and red, and they gleamed like a row of jelly jars.

He paced back and forth in front of them. "Some of you have been asking questions about Camp Hawthorne, especially after your exciting bus ride here."

There was a low murmur from the audience. Everyone else must have had ideas like Lindsey and me.

"Camp Hawthorne was founded years ago by Nathaniel Hawthorne. Some of you may have heard of him." He took a book from the shelf with the title in large gold letters, and I caught the words *Seven Gables*. "He lived in the nineteenth century and wrote some of the best classics in American literature, but he had a secret. His great-great-grandfather was one of the judges at the Salem witch trials."

The murmuring in the room abruptly stopped.

"He changed the spelling of his name so that no one would know they were related. You see, in Hawthorne's day, people were beginning to learn a lot from science, and he realized that the phenomenon from the days of the Salem witch trials wasn't witchcraft. It was a type of ESP or extra-sensory perception."

He paused and the whispering started up again. "What does he mean?" hissed Ellen.

"Cool," Freddy said.

Mr. Parker waved the book in his hand and waited for us to quiet down. "Nathaniel Hawthorne felt so much remorse at the part his family played in the Salem witch trials that he started this camp to protect those with ESP and help them develop their gifts. And that's why you're all here."

He looked at us with an unblinking stare. No one wanted to look at each other. Was he serious? Or was this an elaborate joke for first year campers?

Ellen's face was twisting in a funny way.

Lindsey cocked her head to one side as though listening for something far away. "I knew it," she said softly. She leaned toward me across Ellen. "I've had this feeling for a while."

Ellen shoved her back. "Quiet, I want to hear what he's saying."

"Your bus ride here was an example of teleportation. Our drivers have a kind of ESP that can transfer long distances through tunnels. We have students from every state including Alaska and Hawaii." He beamed as though he was telling us there would be ice cream sundaes for everyone. I realized I was holding my breath, and I let it out slowly.

"We have prepared activities for you each day," Mr. Parker continued. "Activities that we hope will expose your gifts."

Buckeye bounded forward with his guitar. "Shall we have another rousing chorus of the camp song?" he asked with a crazy gleam in his eye.

Our second attempt wasn't as good as our first try. Everyone must have been too bewildered by the news we'd just gotten. Part of me was crowing with delight that Ellen was wrong, and Lindsey and I were right. But then, where were we really? And could we trust Mr. Parker's story? I didn't feel like I had any unusual gift. A flicker of doubt leapt up inside me. What if my invitation was a mistake? My chest was so heavy it was hard to sing.

Next to me, Ellen sat with her brow furrowed, her eyes darting back and forth across the row of books, like she was trying to read their contents. On her other side, Lindsey stared into space as she sang.

I needed to talk to someone. I looked for Jayden and found him edging toward the back. Perhaps he would have some answers.

"Dear Old Camp Hawthorne," Buckeye sang with a final strum. "Assembly is dismissed."

Jayden was almost out the door when I caught up with him. "Can we talk?"

He shoved his hands in his pockets, but he didn't give me his usual scowl. "Let's get outside first, Stella. Too many people."

I started with my questions before we even cleared the porch. "What did Mr. Parker say to you?"

"It was the dishes thing. He told me I have a gift for controlling objects."

"Do you think it's true?"

He frowned. "I thought he was crazy at first, but then he had me shoot some arrows and catch some stuff, and it was all easy."

I had a picture of Jayden shooting baskets at the rickety old hoop in front of his house. "That's why you're so good at basketball," I said.

He shrugged. "Grandma Charlotte used to say something like that, about a gift."

I took a deep breath. I had to say it or I'd never have the guts to say it again. "What if there isn't anything like that for me? Did Mr. Parker say what happens if someone doesn't have a gift?"

"All I know is what he told us at the meeting."

The others caught up with us and wanted to hear Jayden's story again. Even the boys from Bromley wanted to hear, and they hadn't known him that long. Jayden clammed up. "Stella can tell you," he mumbled.

Lindsey was impressed hearing about his gift, but Ellen folded her arms and her eyes narrowed. "It's probably a hoax," she said.

"There's an easy way to find out," I said. "Freddy, you can tell us our coordinates on the GPS, and we can find a map to show us where we are."

"It won't work," he said. "We took our starting location as a waypoint for our hike, but when we got back it changed. Garrett says someone is scrambling the signal in this area." He pulled on the string around his neck and brought out his GPS.

"Wait, what do you mean by scrambling?" That was Lindsey. From the way she acted, you'd think GPS was more amazing than ESP.

"It' a way to mix the signal in sensitive areas. The U.S. military developed it." Freddy held the GPS receiver above his head. "Sometimes you get a better reading if you hold it up."

Buckeye strolled up and fired a shiny smile at us. "Garrett, I was meaning to ask you—what you said in the game—you didn't really bring a GPS, did you?"

Freddy flushed and held out the medallion.

"Sorry," Buckeye said, "I should've thought of that since you're a geo-caching team. But no cell phones or electronic devices allowed at camp. It's for the protection of everyone here."

Buckeye took the GPS like it was a deadly scorpion and buttoned it into his shirt pocket. "I'll return it before you leave for home." He moved on to chat with another group of campers.

"Did you see that?" Ellen said. "It's like he didn't want us to know."

 handwriting-style ornament

CHAPTER EIGHT

ornament

Dinner that night was New England clam chowder. I'd never tasted anything so delicious. Every table had a basket of oyster crackers for sprinkling in the soup. It had a salty smell that reminded me of the time Grandma took me to the beach. I thought of the way Grandma looked when I told her about Mr. Parker's comment to "expect the unexpected." Did she guess there would be something like this? Perhaps she knew more about Camp Hawthorne than she told me. After all, her own daughter attended camp all those years ago.

Ellen was unusually quiet during the meal. I figured part of her wanted to believe, but she was too stubborn to admit it.

"I wonder what my gift will be," Lindsey said.

Jayden was shoveling chowder in his mouth. "Maybe you have a gift for wearing crazy socks."

She looked down at her feet—one turquoise sock and one orange sock. I'd stopped noticing things like that about her a long time ago.

"It *is* a gift," Lindsey said, smiling happily as she dipped a cracker in her chowder and popped it in her mouth.

After dark we roasted marshmallows and stuck them together with chocolate and graham crackers. Ellen couldn't believe I'd never heard of "s'mores."

"I didn't know about them either," Lindsey said. "Until my little sister fell in love with s'mores cereal."

Jayden was pulling his marshmallow off the stick. "They put this stuff in cereal? That's even weirder than ESP."

My marshmallow burned, and I slipped off the blackened crust. The gooey part melted the chocolate bar and got all over my fingers, but it was lovely. Had my parents eaten s'mores like this? I breathed in the wood smoke and listened to the pulsing chorus of frogs. My parents must've heard the same sounds. I thought of the strange warning in the white envelope and realized I had no intentions of taking the advice. Camp Hawthorne was bringing me closer to my parents than I'd ever been in my life. If there was a way to find out more about them, I was going to do it.

We sat on the outer ring of logs around the campfire under the brightest stars I'd ever seen. I felt as though I'd been transported to a different planet in a different galaxy. Even Jayden seemed different out here under the stars— more relaxed, like before he got so quiet.

Ellen peered up at the sky. "Hey Jayden, weren't you telling me about the Big Dipper?"

He tossed his basketball skyward and caught it again. "It's right there." He pointed above our heads to a trail of seven stars.

Buckeye was leading the rest of the campers in a rowdy chorus of some song we hadn't learned yet. "O they built the ship Titanic, to sail the ocean blue…" I didn't even mind that we were new and didn't know how things were done at camp.

"Jayden, do you know any more constellations?" I asked.

He showed us how to find Venus, which looked like a bright star near the horizon, even though it was really a planet.

"Your name means star," he added.

"I didn't think regular old names had meanings," I said.

"Everything has meaning." He tilted back his head to gaze at the stars.

If everything had meaning, maybe there was a reason we were here. Even Ellen.

❧

Lindsey and I made our way back to Hawthorne House by the glow of her flashlight. A cool breeze sprang up, rustling the branches of the Hawthorne elm. Feeling full of marshmallows and chocolate, I climbed the stairs behind her.

I was following her into our room when she stopped with a gasp. Her light flickered over our bunk, which looked like an explosion site. Everything I'd packed for camp was scattered on the floor and over our beds—T-shirts, socks, jeans, even my paper and stamps to write home. She found the light switch and turned it on. My clothesline hung from the bunk like an abandoned spider web and the butterfly net had a gaping hole torn in it.

Tears smarted in my eyes as I stooped to pick it up.

"Who would do this?" Lindsey said, scooping up clothes by the armful.

I glanced over at Joanne's bed, smugly neat, her designer jeans stacked in bins. "I bet I know." I crammed everything back in my suitcase, not even caring if they were folded or not.

Lindsey found my toothbrush under the bunk. "I'll wash off the dust for you."

I picked up the picture of my parents, but the frame was empty. Waves of tiredness washed over me, and my arms felt too heavy to move. "Never mind, we can find the rest of the stuff tomorrow."

It was too much effort to put the sheets back on my bed. I draped them over me with my sleeping bag at my feet, and turned my face toward the wall.

I wasn't even at camp a full day, and already I had an enemy. I squeezed my eyes tight to keep the tears from leaking through. I thought camp would be all about fun and making new friends, but it was turning out to be something very different. I'd been holding my breath, and I let it out in a shaky sigh. Grandma used to say "tomorrow is another day." I hoped she was right.

CHAPTER NINE

The next morning I woke up to the sound of a creaky bugle sounding a few feet from my ear. The sun shone through the windows, casting hazy shadows on my wall. The bugle stopped and several girls groaned.

"Special K!" It was Joanne's voice, sharp and shrill. A thump and a clatter followed. I rolled over and saw a skinny girl in jeans and a blue T-shirt lifting a bugle from the floor.

"And give me my pillow back," Joanne shouted.

The girl picked up the pillow and put it on Joanne's bed. "I thought I was a member of the band," she said softly.

"Yeah, when we have band practice. Not at sunrise." Joanne grabbed her pillow and stuffed it over her head.

I noticed a small cluster of things I hadn't found last night arranged in a circle at the foot of my bed. The skinny girl picked up a stray sock and added it to the collection. "Some of your stuff was flung around," she said.

"Thanks." For a moment the misery of last evening rushed back.

"And look, I fixed your butterfly net." She swished it back and forth.

I had to swallow before I could speak. The net looked even better than when Grandma first found it for me. "How'd you do that?"

"Simple telekinesis," she said.

"Is that why they call you Special K?"

"No, that's only Joanne. I'm Karen." She leaned the butterfly net by the cot. "Cecily sent me to wake up the girls' dorm." She glanced at Joanne and giggled. "I have a plan for the ones who don't wake up the first time."

I wondered if this was a normal occurrence at camp. "I better wake up Lindsey and Ellen. We're first year campers."

"I know." Karen drifted toward the hallway. "You'll want to get your friends and get dressed before it happens."

I gave Lindsey a shake, knowing it would take her a few tries to wake up. Ellen was curled up in a ball, but sat up when I said her name. "We have to get out before something happens," I said.

She looked at me strangely before reaching for her shoes.

I kept calling Lindsey's name while I pulled on my clothes, and she finally opened her eyes.

"Morning already?"

Karen popped her head around the doorway. "Time to get out—now!" Something in her tone made us scramble. Lindsey hopped off the bunk, and we ran for the door. Karen closed it firmly and led us to the shower room. "You'll be safe in here."

Ellen shook her head. "What is this..." she began, when an explosion of noise broke out in the dormitory. A bass drum boomed, a bugle sounded, and girls screamed. The metal bunks clanked back and forth as a dozen feet pounded across the floor. The door banged open, and I heard something like fireworks. Joanne shouted, "Special K—"

"Better go," Karen whispered. She opened a door to a set of back stairs and raced down to a room where a huge brick fireplace took up one wall.

Lindsey was already wearing jeans and a T-shirt.

"You slept in your clothes?" I asked, as we dashed out the door and past the giant elm.

"It makes things faster in the morning."

We ran until we reached the Junction Stone, then Karen stopped and doubled over with laughter. "Wasn't that great?"

"I'd call it dangerous," Ellen said, her arms folded.

Karen wiped tears from her eyes. "No, it was only a special Karen multi-media presentation. Fireworks, bass drums, the works."

"How'd you do it?" I asked.

She flashed a mysterious smirk. "Trade secret. But let that be a lesson to everyone to get up on the first bugle call. Now it's time for breakfast."

❦

The boys joined us in the dining hall a few minutes later. "Did you hear the explosion?" Jayden asked.

"Eugene told us to come here while he checked it out," said Freddy, whose hair was sticking up. I suspected he didn't have time to comb it before he left. "Do you know what it was?"

I opened my mouth to say something, but Karen interrupted. "It must have been a welcome-to-camp thing," she said airily. "You'll notice that everyone from Hawthorne House arrived for breakfast on time."

It was true. Joanne and the other girls from our dorm were straggling in, rubbing their ears and staring angrily in our direction. Karen ducked behind a box of cereal. "Let me know when they're safely seated," she muttered.

The girls sat at another table, and Joanne turned her back to us. "It's safe now," I said.

She sat up again with a satisfied smile. "That will give us ten points for Hawthorne House—"

"Ten points?" I asked.

Karen was passing cereal bowls around the table as though nothing remarkable had just happened. "The dorms compete for points, which you get for good inspections and being on time."

"Or for winning the daily challenge," added Eugene. He had an amazing ability to sneak up on us. He was wearing all-black again today.

Sitting in the remaining chair, he poured himself a bowl of cereal. "Good work, Karen. Hawthorne House is in the lead." His flat voice held a tinge of energy as he motioned to a poster next to the fireplace. Buckeye was adding a star in the row marked "Thornes."

"I don't get it," I said.

"There are five dorms here," he replied. "All replicas of the houses of Hawthorne and his friends. They helped start our camp—Longfellow, Whittier, Alcott and Twain."

Jayden was sitting across from me, and his eyebrows shot up.

"What?" I said to him. I wondered if he could read minds as well as control objects.

"They're authors," he explained. "Henry Wadsworth Longfellow, John Greenleaf Whittier, Louisa May Alcott and Mark Twain."

"Literature is *not* dead," Eugene said.

Ellen put down her orange juice. "Why would they help with camp?"

"You have to read what they wrote," he said. "They knew ESP was real, and Hawthorne got them to support his work. Our dorms are named for them as a tribute."

Lindsey squinted at the poster. "So we're called the Thornes, and the others are the Fellows, the Whits, the Alcotts and the Twains?"

"Well done." Cecily appeared at our table bearing a platter of pancakes. "I wondered what happened to your runner," she said. "Y'all eat up now. Buckeye has big plans for you today, and the Thornes need to stay number one."

Eugene growled. He was certainly a strange one.

≪જ૭

CHAPTER TEN

≪જ૭

After breakfast Skeeter was waiting for us at the lake. "Welcome to swim certification, campers—you're going to get in groups of three and swim to the buoy."

I groaned, and unfortunately Ellen heard me. "What's wrong. Can't you swim?" she asked.

I shook my head. "I never learned."

"Me neither," Jayden said. "But it doesn't look too hard."

I watched Skeeter wading out to the buoy and hoped I wouldn't drown before I reached her. It didn't look too deep. The boys from Bromley took off in the first group, and the rest of us got in the water to wait our turn. The first shock of cold almost sent me back to the beach, but I gritted my teeth and stood next to Lindsey. I knew she took lessons at the community pool. "Can you teach me real fast?" I asked her.

She bobbed down into the water. "Try this." She brought her arms up to her chest and made a scooping motion to the side. I tried making the motion in the air and hoped it wouldn't be my turn until the sun got hotter.

Skeeter blew her whistle. "Next group!"

Another boy splashed forward, and Joanne and her friend joined him, speeding through the water like sharks on attack.

Karen watched them and bit her lip. "That's why Joanne calls me Special K. I can't swim, even with lessons at home. Nothing helps."

I stepped in a little deeper. I was getting used to the freezing water. "What happens if you can't swim?"

"You have to skip craft class and take swim lessons till you learn or they give up on you."

"What do you mean—*give up on you?*"

"I flunked three times last year before they gave up and let me get on with craft classes." Karen shrugged. "Swimming's not important for most of us. Lots of people with ESP naturally float. See." She sat back in the water, but she didn't sink. She just lay on the surface, thrashing her arms.

The whistle blew, and Lindsey took off with Jayden and Ellen. Ellen shot ahead doing a windmill stroke. Jayden watched her and circled his arms the same way so that the two of them looked like twin engines. Lindsey followed slowly, doing her scooping motion.

"We should go next," Karen said. She splashed along on her back. "Get in, see if you float, too."

I lowered myself into the lake and felt the icy water flowing around me. It reminded me of the statistics for drowning—lifetime risk: one in nine thousand. I was wondering if I should be worried, when my legs rose up from under me. "I'm floating!"

"Of course, silly. Now get moving."

Rolling onto my front with my head above water, I tried Lindsey's swim stroke. I didn't go very fast, but I easily kept pace with Karen as she puttered forward.

"Swimming isn't so bad," I said.

Karen gave me a funny look. "Prepare yourself. Skeeter might not call this swimming."

One of the other girls sped past us and quickly joined the "certified group" standing next to Skeeter.

"Good job," Lindsey called when we arrived at last.

"You're water-safe," Skeeter said, "but you'd both benefit from lessons. You two stand on the other side."

Karen locked arms with me and stalked away from the certified group. "Come on, Stella. You'd rather hang out with me anyway."

More campers joined us on the next round. Karen introduced me to two girls named Annalisa and Destiny and a boy in purple swim trunks called Ivan. "He's the only one who came from his school," she explained. "The other teammates got chicken pox at the last minute."

"That's strange," I said. "Most kids get vaccines for chicken pox when they're little."

Ivan's ears turned red. "Lots of people in my community don't believe in vaccines."

I would have asked him more, but Skeeter joined us. "Welcome to swim class."

While the others had a free swim, she made us float on our stomachs and put our faces in the water to blow bubbles. Then she made us turn our heads to the side to take a breath. I kept choking on the water, and I don't think Karen ever took a real breath at all. Whenever she wanted to breathe she stood up to inhale and then went back to floating.

"No, Karen," yelled Skeeter. "You won't be able to stand up in the middle of the lake."

I looked over at Annalisa and Destiny, who seemed to be getting it. I tried again, and I actually took a breath without gargling water.

"Good," Skeeter called out. "Now try kicking your legs."

By the end of the lesson, most of us could make windmills with our arms and kick a little. I was pleased with my progress, but Karen wore a sour expression. "You'll learn to swim and leave me like all the others."

"Don't you want to learn so you won't miss craft class?" I asked.

"Huh—it's not crafts like you're used to. Craft classes are where we develop our gifts."

I kicked my feet, enjoying the new feeling of floating in water. "What's your gift?"

"I can move things."

"That's the same as Jayden. What's class like?"

"We start small with juggling or archery. Then we progress to tying shoe laces and picking locks."

"Picking locks? Isn't that illegal?"

"Not if you don't use it to steal something."

"Is that how you made the explosion this morning?"

Karen hugged herself and started laughing. "It was tremendous—I used every trick they taught us."

I wondered why they would teach things like that.

❧

By the time our swim lesson finished, the CITs appeared, carrying huge boxes which they lined up on the shore.

Karen waded out of the water. "Hurry up—it's a picnic lunch."

The breeze blew cool across the lake, and I ran for my towel, while Karen grabbed two lunch bags from the box marked "V."

"Vegetarian," she said. "Better than lunch meat."

We sat on a log by the fire circle. Though the fire was gone, the memory of last night with the stars and s'mores brought a quivery feeling of belonging. I opened my bag and found a sandwich made from squishy orange stuff between two slices of brown bread. I tried a bit with the tip of my tongue, and it was salty.

"Pimento cheese," Karen said.

I took a small bite. The brown bread was thick and chewy, and the pimento cheese was tangy and smooth. I hadn't realized how hungry I was, and my sandwich disappeared in two minutes flat. Smaller packages contained peanuts, carrots and a brownie, which I was just finishing when the others arrived.

"The vegetarian ones were gone," Lindsey moaned.

"I'll take the bologna, and you can eat the bread," Jayden said.

"Gross," Ellen squawked, as she opened her sandwich and peeled off the meat.

Jayden made a triple-stack of bologna on bread and held it up for us to admire, waving it like he was a fancy chef. "Just like Grandma Charlotte makes."

Memories of eating bologna sandwiches in his grandmother's kitchen rolled through my brain. "Super-duper bologna sandwiches" we used to call them. We'd only been at camp two days, but Jayden seemed more like his old self, and I was glad.

"Listen up, campers." Buckeye scanned the crowd until he had absolute silence. "Every day we'll have an activity so the first year campers can find their gifts. We're beginning with the second annual treasure hunt, and to add a little excitement, you'll compete as dorms."

There were groans from campers. "Not again, Buckeye," someone wailed.

"Wasn't last year enough?" another voice rang out.

"What happened last year?" I whispered to Karen.

She just smiled.

"Healthy competition," Buckeye said. "You know the drill—everyone help each other so no one gets hurt."

"What if we get hurt?" That was Joanne.

Buckeye ignored her. "This year's treasure hunt is by canoe." He held up a bunch of keys dangling from cords. "These beauties will unlock your treasure chest, but don't be fooled. There are lots of false trails and only a few true ones, so beware."

Joanne and her crew looked our way, nudging each other and laughing.

Buckeye raised his voice over the chatter. "Your mission is to paddle to the island and locate your next packet. Follow the clues until you find your treasure chest, and unlock it with your key. Bring whatever's inside to me."

Eugene appeared out of nowhere. "Newbies are on my team." He rounded up the boys from Bromley and Ivan in the purple swim trunks. He had tied his T-shirt around his head like a pirate. "Huddle up," he said, motioning us to come in closer. "They've put the new campers from Hawthorne House on team three, which means no one expects us to win. But we'll show them."

"Yeah!" said Ivan.

"First thing, who knows how to paddle?"

Freddy, Coop and Garrett raised their hands.

"Good. You'll man the front and back positions. I'll help in the middle."

Eugene led us to the beach, where the canoes bobbed at the water's edge. I hadn't realized how long they were. They had four benches and one short seat tucked up at the back of the boat. Buckeye was there with his clipboard, handing out paddles.

Mine had faded red paint like the one my parents held in the photograph. I gripped the handle and imagined my mother had held this same paddle once.

Jayden stepped toward one of the canoes, but Buckeye waved his hands wildly. "Not till we get everyone in life vests!"

The orange vest, shaped like a horseshoe, hugged my neck. The straps were still wet from the last person who used it, and they flapped like slimy tendrils against my legs.

Eugene waded into the water and steadied the canoe. "Get in one by one."

Garrett and Coop went first, hunched low and scurrying to the front seat like ninjas. I was impressed.

"Beginners, next," Eugene said.

Lindsey jumped aboard, and the boat lurched back and forth.

He winced. "Stay low so you don't capsize the boat."

Jayden followed her without disturbing the balance.

"You go next," Ivan said, gripping his paddle nervously. "I haven't figured it out yet."

Though I tried to keep low, we would have capsized if Jayden hadn't leaned to the side. I plopped onto the bench next to Lindsey and turned toward Ivan. "Come on—it's not so bad."

His face as white as the paper on Buckeye's clipboard, Ivan stepped into the boat and collapsed in the direction of an empty bench. When he realized he was safe, he punched his fist in the air. "I did it!"

The others came aboard, sitting two to a row with Freddy perched expectantly on the last seat. By now most of the canoes had pulled out ahead of us.

Ellen raised her hand. "Did Buckeye say this was a competition?"

For answer, Eugene dug his paddle in the lake. "Time to go," he barked. "Sweep your paddles like this." The others followed his directions, and we glided through the water toward the weedy island.

I was the only person not rowing, and Eugene passed me the key. "Keep this safe," he muttered—like he was giving me a top-secret mission.

I hung the key around my neck, then dipped my paddle to match the others. The sun was directly above us, and the warmth on my skin made my arms tingle with pure joy as the boat surged forward. If this was canoeing, I was going to like it.

After his initial fright, Ivan began to relax and enjoy himself. With his long arms, he plunged his paddle deep in the water, and we shot ahead. "I have a feeling we're going to win," he said.

Just then a droning murmur came from behind us. It was the Fellows' canoe. They were chanting in unison:

By the shores of Gitche Gumee,
By the shining Big-Sea-Water...

Their paddles swept in time with the words, and sparkles of water dropped from their blades. I stopped paddling to watch.

Stood the wigwam of Nokomis,
Daughter of the Moon, Nokomis.

The canoe cut through the lake as their murmuring hum grew louder.

Jayden leaned toward me. "That's from a poem by Longfellow."

"Back to paddling," roared Eugene. I wrenched my eyes from the speeding canoe and tried to get back into sync with the rest of the boat.

> *Rose the firs with cones upon them;*
> *Bright before it beat the water,*
> *Beat the clear and sunny water,*
> *Beat the shining Big-Sea-Water.*

The Fellows' canoe finally disappeared around the edge of the island. I took a deep breath and looked around with new eyes. Shining waters. That was just right. I thought of my parents canoeing on this lake, ringed with fir trees and blue sky. I could drift here forever.

"Hold up," Eugene barked. "Time to make our strategy. Stella, read the tag on our key."

I jerked out of my thoughts and fumbled for the piece of cardboard. "Thorne Team #3: South harbor, oak tree dead ahead, fifth branch up," I read.

"We head for the tip of the island there." Eugene pointed to the right.

Freddy, from his place at the back, piped up. "Shouldn't we have a cool chant like the Fellows so we can keep time?"

Eugene seemed torn. "Good idea, but we can't waste time learning one now."

"Why don't you say it for us?" I asked.

His face reddened. "All right, but you have to give it your all. This one's by Hawthorne."

I didn't know what to expect, so I was surprised when his voice rang out deep and strong:

Oh, earthly pomp is but a dream,
And like a meteor's short-lived gleam;

He plunged his paddle through the water, and we followed his motion.

And all the sons of glory soon
Will rest beneath the mould'ring stone.

Everyone made their strokes in time with the lines, and our canoe sped forward.

And Genius is a star whose light
Is soon to sink in endless night,
And heavenly beauty's angel form
Will bend like flower in winter's storm.

The thrilling words and clash of paddles sent prickles down my arms. We skimmed across the lake, and a few minutes later our canoe ran up onto the beach with a crunching of loose pebbles.

Everyone cheered, and Eugene jumped from the boat to pull it above the water line. The applause faded when we saw Joanne running toward us. She fluttered a piece of paper in the air as her crew pulled away. "Better luck next time!"

In the bright sunlight her face seemed to wobble back and forth. I pressed my eyes shut for a moment. When I looked again, the double-vision was gone. I hoped I wasn't getting sick.

Eugene planted his paddle in the sand, and the muscle in his jaw tightened. "It's not over yet," he said. "South harbor, oak tree dead ahead, fifth branch."

Freddy took off with Coop and Garret right behind him, like a pack of beagles on the hunt. "Dead ahead," he shouted. He reached the tree first and swung himself up into the branches.

"Nothing here."

"Did you start at the right place?" Ellen called.

Freddy pulled out his compass and squinted back at the beach. "You're right. The southernmost point is over there." He swept his arm from the shoreline to a stand of oaks. Garret took off, and Coop followed him. They were soon jumping up and down and pointing to a package hanging from a tree. One after the other, they shinnied up the trunk.

"Wait," Freddy shouted. "Something's wrong."

But they didn't hear him. Garrett scooted out along the branch and pulled the wrapping from the packet. There was a pop, and a cloud of purple ink sprayed him in the face. He teetered and barely saved himself from falling by catching hold of a limb.

"Safety protocol," Freddy yelled, sprinting toward them. "Keep your eyes closed."

He whipped out his water bottle and passed it up to Coop, who used it to rinse Garrett's eyes. His face was splotchy with the remnants of purple ink, but he gave us a thumbs-up sign.

Eugene shook his head. "That must have been one of the false clues." He peered at Freddy. "How'd you know something was wrong?"

"I just knew. It was like I could see the packet, and our name wasn't on it."

"Let's try an experiment," Eugene said. "There's a clue around here that's marked for us. Close your eyes and see if you can find it."

Freddy tilted back his head and closed his eyes like some kind of sun-worshipper. The freckles on his face stood out darker and more numerous than ever. Slowly, he turned. "Joanne got the wrong clue—hers is over there." He rotated a little farther. "And there's our clue." He pointed to a tree closer to the shore.

Eugene made the boys go more carefully this time. They removed the packet from the branch and handed it to him. It was labeled *Thorne Team #3*.

I realized we'd just witnessed something amazing— Freddy had an incredible talent. Eugene clapped him on the back. "You've got the gift for reading hidden writing," he said. He let Freddy open the packet. It contained a hand-drawn map with an X marked on the far shore and the words *great rock* penciled above it.

"Cool," Freddy said.

"Let's go," Eugene growled.

CHAPTER ELEVEN

We raced back to our canoe. Cecily's team was just paddling into shore. They were laughing and joking, and two of their members were overboard, hanging onto the side.

"Hey Eugene," called Cecily. "Having fun yet?"

He stiffened. "We got our packet, so we're looking good. Beware of false clues—they're using ink bombs this year."

"Thanks partner," she replied, and a few of the kids whooped in appreciation.

Karen offered me a feeble wave. "We're the party team," she said. "Don't expect us for dinner."

The rest of her crew laughed. I wanted to stop and visit, but Eugene jumped in the canoe. "Gotta go," he barked.

"Our crew is more like the Marines," I told Lindsey.

Ellen jabbed me in the shoulder with her paddle. "Don't you want to win, Stella?"

I sighed and gripped my paddle. If I could, I'd let the splashing paddles and sparkling lake take me into a dream world.

Freddy launched the canoe, and Eugene started up our chant. *"Oh, earthly pomp is but a dream, and like a meteor's short-lived gleam."*

"Faster," roared Ellen.

Racing from the island, we made for the gray rock on the far side of the lake. Eugene was so excited that he kept pushing the pace of the chant. Jayden sliced his paddle through the water like a machine, and even Lindsey and I were getting the hang of it.

The closer we got to the rock, the larger it grew, until I realized it was actually a cave. The canoe glided under the overhanging stone, and the sunlight reflected back from the shallow bottom making the ceiling shimmer.

"Freddy, any feel for where the next clue is?" Eugene's voice sounded hollow.

Freddy closed his eyes. "It seems to be up there, but that doesn't make sense."

"Wait," Jayden said. "I see something." He stood and pulled himself up to a shelf that ran along one side of the cave. From there he crawled toward the patch where Freddy was pointing. "There's moss here, but it's fake." A shower of dust fell on those in the front of the canoe, and everyone cheered.

He tossed the packet to Eugene, who looked at Freddy before opening it.

"It's safe," he said.

Eugene read the clue aloud. "Thorne Team #3: Find the first tribute-ary. Unlock the chest under the great elm." He held it up for us to see. "Tributary is spelled funny."

"Does this lake have a tributary?" Freddy asked. He paddled backwards to ease us out of the cave.

I bent all my concentration on the clue, positive I'd heard that word "tribute" somewhere today.

As we left the cave, a voice from above cried "aha!" The paper tore from Eugene's grasp and soared above our heads toward the top of the rock, where a brown hand pulled it out of the air.

"What in the world—" Ellen began, but stopped as the canoe began to shake.

"Quick," Eugene shouted. "Paddle everyone!"

Some of us pulled one way and some the other, and the canoe wobbled crazily. We were going to capsize any minute, and my heart clutched in terror.

Lindsey didn't even try to row. She clung to the boat and shrieked with laughter. "Woohoo!" she said over and over, until Eugene fixed her with his dark glare, and she put her paddle back into motion.

"Pull to the right," he shouted, and we turned around at last.

The boat quickly navigated into smooth waters, but my hands were shaking. There seemed to be a tiny step in adventures between fun and scary. I figured the probability of dying from canoe accidents was up there with death by heart attack. I wished I could be like Lindsey and enjoy the moment, but I was too busy fearing we'd drown.

When we got far enough from the cave, Eugene called a stop. "Listen up, Thornes." He talked so low we had to lean toward him. "It's against the rules, but it happens sometimes—a pirate team is trying to sabotage our mission or use our clue, or both." He paused to let that sink in. "We've got to figure out the clue before they do, and use it to our advantage."

"Let's look at the map," Freddy said.

Garrett, his face still purple from the ink, spread it out for us. "This might be a tributary here."

Coop shook his head. "More like an inlet."

Now that we were back in the sunlight, my double vision returned. Garrett seemed to have two purple heads, one slightly behind the other. I closed my eyes and tried to concentrate on the clue. Perhaps the key would help. I pulled on the cord around my neck and held the key in my palm. When I opened my eyes, my vision was normal again. The tag read: *Thorne Team #3*. It reminded me of what Karen told us at breakfast—how our dormitories were named as a *tribute* to the people who started the camp. "Tribute!" I shouted. "Remember how it's spelled strange? It's talking about Hawthorne House— built in tribute to Hawthorne."

"And it was the first," Eugene said.

"And there's a lovely elm tree," added Lindsey.

Eugene looked around to make sure no one was listening, which seemed pretty silly since we were in the middle of the lake. "We're going to convince them we're looking in that inlet," he whispered. "Here's the plan."

I wasn't wild about the plan, mainly because I would have to swim. But, as Lindsey pointed out, I should be fine with the life jacket. We were going to paddle around the island until we were close to shore and hidden from the pirates. Then Lindsey, Ellen and I would swim back and find the real clue. The rest of the team would canoe to the inlet and pretend to search. "We won't beat the Fellows," said Eugene, "but we can do everything possible to trick those pirates."

While Lindsey swam serenely by my side, Ellen coached my swimming. "Kick with your feet—don't thrash your arms like that." By a combination of nagging and demonstration, she got me to the beach. I wanted to flop on the sand for a rest, but Ellen had caught Eugene's gung-ho spirit. "Faster," she said, as we hustled up the trail. We even jogged the dirt track to the Junction Stone. I was ready to collapse and send the others ahead when Karen stepped from behind the stone.

"What are you doing here?" she asked.

Ellen's eyes narrowed. "Are you the one who stole our clue?" She didn't wait for an answer but kept fast-walking toward our dorm.

Karen jogged after us. "No. Someone took our clue too, and we've got off the rest of the afternoon."

Ellen kept going.

"Hey, you're still following your clue, aren't you?" Karen ran ahead and planted herself in the path.

"Of course," I said. "You should come with us. Your clue might be with ours."

Ellen stared daggers at me, but I had a feeling I was right. "More points for the Thornes."

Ellen dodged around Karen. "All right, but you have to let us go first."

Giving us a considering nod, Karen pulled the cord around her neck. "Cecily was right to give the key to me."

At Hawthorne House, we spread out around the base of the elm tree.

"Nothing here," Lindsey called.

I didn't see anything at first, but then I scraped away some dry leaves and found a plaque sunk in the ground. "Look at this—*In tribute to Nathaniel Hawthorne, this tree was planted July 4, 1874.*" The earth next to the plaque was still soft. Someone had dug there recently.

"You need help," said Karen, motioning with her hand. A shovel floated through the air from a box beside the front door.

My arms found new energy, and I dug as quickly as I could while Ellen supervised. The shovel hit something hard. "It's here!" The others joined me in scooping back the dirt. We uncovered a cluster of three boxes, shaped like miniature pirate's chests with numbers etched in the brass straps.

"Open box number three," Ellen said, jigging with impatience. The key fit the lock, and inside lay a pure white rose with a single thorn.

"I'll take it to Buckeye right away," she crowed, before disappearing down the path at a full sprint.

Lindsey and I sat and watched Karen dig out her box. "You saw our team," she said. "We weren't going to win a prize, but then someone levitated our clue right out of Cecily's hand. It made me mad, especially when the others thought it was a big joke." A slow smile crept across her face as she slipped the key in the lock. "But there are other ways to win. I put a mud-pulling telekinesis on our clue as it fluttered away. Whoever gets it will be covered in mud the next time you see them." She opened the lid and took out a blood-red rose. "I'll just walk this to Buckeye, shall I?"

I shivered a little as I watched Karen go, and it wasn't from my wet swimsuit.

≪≫

CHAPTER TWELVE

≪≫

Half-way through dinner, Joanne and her crew trailed in, covered with mud and bits of leaves. Joanne threw the crumpled clue at me as she passed our table. "If you hadn't gotten in the way, the Thornes would have made a respectable win," she hissed.

I looked up at the score board. Two Thorne canoes came in fifth and sixth, not bad considering the sabotage. The Fellows won, of course. It's hard to beat the kind of team spirit that has its own paddling chant.

Mr. Parker called for attention at the end of the meal. "Congratulations to everyone on a well-played treasure hunt."

The Fellows clapped and cheered, and Eugene gave the girls at our table a thumbs-up sign.

Maybe his competitive spirit was contagious, because I felt like I was glowing inside.

"Just wait for the next competition," he said. "The Thornes will really shine."

Mr. Parker continued. "We have a few announcements. First, the clairvoyant group is inviting everyone to play cards at Longfellow House tonight. Decks of cards will be provided."

"Our dorm can go together," Karen whispered.

"Second, I want to remind all of you that even if you have a telekinetic at your table, you must accompany your dishes to the wash bins. We can't have dishes seeming to wash themselves."

Someone at Joanne's table gave a bark of laughter, and Mr. Parker glanced in their direction, but by then everyone was bent over the food.

"Finally, as you know, our mission here is to train you in the use of your gifts, but we also want to prepare you to return to the regular world. That's why we recruit you as teams. When you return home, you will help each other use your abilities in a responsible way and keep them hidden as much as possible. Above all, for the safety of everyone here, Camp Hawthorne must be kept a secret. We are trusting you." His gaze swept the room, and then his face brightened. "And now it is customary to share some words of wisdom from our benefactors, as a kind of tribute."

Most of the campers got the double meaning of the last word, and whispers rippled through the room.

"Tonight I'd like to read a quote from Nathaniel Hawthorne as recorded in *The House of Seven Gables.*" He cleared his throat and opened a green volume. "Is it a fact—or have I dreamt it—that, by means of electricity, the world of matter has become a great nerve, vibrating thousands of miles in a breathless point of time?" He stopped and closed the book. "Dinner is dismissed."

The boys were reluctant to attend the card party, but Karen convinced everyone to go. She led the way to the Junction Stone, and instead of taking the left path to our dorm, she took the path straight ahead. After seeing the homes of Twain and Hawthorne, I was eager to visit Longfellow House. Except for the canoe chant, I didn't know anything about him.

Karen led us around a curve, and I caught sight of the house, glowing in the light of the setting sun. It sat on a velvet green lawn—a vast yellow building with rows of windows framed with black shutters. Four white columns rose across the front and gave the house an air of majesty.

"Wow, I wonder what it's like to live there," I said.

She snorted. "You have to take turns cutting the grass."

We walked up to one of the wide porches that flanked both sides of the house, where Skeeter was placing decks of cards on the tables. "You're the first to arrive, so go ahead and get started," she said.

Karen scooped up cards from a box marked *Beginners*. "I'll take care of them."

She divided us into groups of four. Freddy, Ellen, Jayden and I ended up at the same table. Karen dealt the cards, which had silly fish printed on them. "Beginners start with *Go Fish*," she said.

I glanced over at Jayden to see if he would balk at playing a baby game, but he was smiling and sorting his cards. He wasn't even carrying his basketball.

We took turns asking each other for matches, and Freddy started winning right away. Jayden amused himself by building a house of cards from the matches Freddy collected. When the card house was eight stories high, Karen swooped in and told us Freddy wasn't a beginner anymore. More campers were arriving, and she transferred him to another table.

Ellen squinted at the cards. "We can do this. Everyone touch a card and see if you get an idea of what it is." I almost burst with concentration, but nothing came. Ellen shook her head. "I get an image but it's too fuzzy."

Karen took the empty seat at our table. "You can't force it," she said. "Let's just have some fun." She brought out a regular deck and taught us how to play spades and then showed Jayden how to deal cards without touching them. Skeeter passed out peanuts and bug juice, and I sat back and listened to the hum of conversation.

Moths fluttered around the porch lights, while deeper in the yard, lightening bugs flashed. I imagined my parents were at camp. They were just inviting me to play cards, when Jayden broke into my dream.

"I won," he said, laying down his last card.

"Huh," said Karen, and a peanut flew up and landed on Jayden's head.

"This what you want?" he replied lazily, and a cup of bug juice glided through the air to hover over Karen's shoulder.

"You wouldn't dare—" But even as she was speaking, the cup tilted and purple juice trickled out. She spluttered, and the entire bowl of peanuts levitated, ready to dash itself at Jayden's face.

Instantly Skeeter was at our table, grabbing the bowl out of the air. "What are you doing?" she demanded. "You think people work hard to run this camp so you can do silly tricks?"

Karen shrank on herself after Skeeter stormed off. "Sorry Jayden. I forgot to tell you—we have our first craft class in telekinetics tomorrow. And Skeeter's our teacher."

CHAPTER THIRTEEN

Everything went wrong the next day from the moment I woke up. To start, Cecily announced a dorm inspection, and Joanne pounced on us and made everyone make their beds before we even got dressed.

"Bedding should be tight as a drum," she said with grim satisfaction, as we smoothed our sleeping bags over the mattresses to hide the wrinkles.

Breakfast was a white mixture Cecily called grits. She suggested I add butter and salt, but it didn't help.

After breakfast everyone who'd found their gifts went to classes. The rest of us had swimming in the lake, but I was stuck with the swim lessons again while Lindsey and Ellen got to play Marco Polo with the others. I'd forgotten everything I learned the day before, and I flailed around in the water, alternately kicking my feet or scooping with my hands. It was a relief when Cecily blew the whistle and told us to report to the dining hall for lunch.

Karen motioned me over to the Thorne table with Cecily and Eugene. "You better eat up," she said. "The new campers are assigned orientation activities today."

"What's that?" I asked.

"It depends on the group. The Fellows are mapping old Indian trails, the Whits are snorkeling on the lake, the Alcotts are rock-climbing, and the Twains are exploring a cave."

"What are we doing?"

"Hiking to a dig site and searching for artifacts with me," Cecily said. She was wearing another Shakespeare T-shirt that read *The first thing we do, let's kill all the lawyers. (Henry VI, Part 2).*

Eugene was teaching a class for older campers, but he urged us to find as much as we could at the dig site. "We've got to earn more points for the Thornes," he said.

We stopped by Hawthorne House after lunch to pick up hats, sunscreen and water bottles. I slung the canteen from Grandma over my shoulder, hoping the others would be impressed by my genuine military equipment. Then I grabbed my cap and my mother's bandana and ran down the stairs to meet the others in the camp store.

Most of the others wore ball caps like mine. The boys from Bromley had red ones with a B monogrammed on them, and Jayden had loaned one of his caps to Ivan. I wondered if Ivan's community didn't believe in baseball, either.

Lindsey had a floppy straw hat, and Ellen had a white hat with flaps. "It's used in the desert for archeological digs," she informed us.

Not to be outdone, I pulled out the bandana. "This is what they used to wear at camp."

"Let me see," Cecily said. "My mother has one just like this—she came to camp, too."

She held it up, and a white piece of paper fell out. I reached for the paper but froze at the sight of block printing—the same lettering as my warning letter. Turning away so the others wouldn't see, I read the words:

STELLA, IT'S DANGEROUS TO PURSUE INFORMATION ABOUT YOUR PARENTS.

I felt dizzy. Who was doing this? Was it a harmless prank or was it serious? How did they find me at camp? Nobody even knew where I was. The thought of the brown people popped in my head, but that was ridiculous. I crumpled the note and stuffed it in my pocket. If someone thought they could scare me away from my parents, they were wrong.

Cecily handed the bandana back, and I tied it around my neck with a tight knot. I fell into step with Lindsey, who immediately noticed something was bothering me.

"You're taking deep breaths again."

"I don't want to talk about it." I let out my breath and tried to forget the note.

We followed Cecily on a path that took us past the lake and up into the hills. She pointed out Aunt Winnie's house, a tiny log cabin almost hidden among the pine trees. I remembered she was the one with the pigs who ate our table scraps, and I searched for the pen, but it must have been on the other side.

While we walked, Jayden and Freddy told us about their morning classes. Jayden learned how to use telekinetics to wash dishes, and Freddy practiced reading hidden writing.

"Buckeye is the teacher," he said. "He's from England, but he's nuts about American authors like Mark Twain. We took turns reading out of a Twain biography while he held the book closed. Did you know Twain himself had ESP? He foretold his brother's death, and he never got over it. Some people believe he was dabbling in time travel because of stuff he wrote."

"Did he ever really travel in time?" Lindsey asked.

"That's just fiction," Ellen said.

"Is it?" Her quiet stare made Ellen blink. "It could be the next great invention," she added. "Like space travel."

Ellen didn't have an answer for that.

The day grew warmer, and Cecily made us stop for a water break. I wasn't sure if my canteen held as much as modern water bottles so I only took a few sips.

At our second break, she gave us some thick brushes she had brought. "We're almost there, and you'll use these when you get close to an artifact," she explained.

"What are we looking for?" Freddy asked.

Cecily hesitated. "This dig site holds some strange objects. In the last twenty years we've unearthed antiquities that never should have been there." She stopped abruptly.

"Like what?" I asked, but she bit down on her lip and changed the subject.

"You can drink the rest of your water now because we have a cistern at the dig site," she said.

The water gave us a spurt of energy for the last stretch up the hill, but when we arrived, everything was a mess. The cistern lay on its side, and a big gash showed where the water had leaked out. Someone had knocked out the boundary stakes, and the strings dividing the plot into sections were limp and twisted.

"No water," groaned Ivan. "What will we do in this heat?"

Cecily frowned. "First we'll fix what someone tried to destroy." She peered up at the sun. "But we may have to go back early."

She assigned us partners so we could stand on either side of the square and tighten the strings. As I knelt in the dirt, I spotted a scrap of paper. It was blank except for a curly signature that appeared to be *Hepzibah*.

I showed it to the others, but Cecily took it away and put it in her pocket. "I need to show this to Mr. Parker," she said.

I glanced at Lindsey—we were thinking the same thing—there was a mystery here that campers weren't supposed to know.

Cecily darted around the edges of the dig site, checking everyone's work. When she was satisfied the site was in order, she took out a diagram showing a grid marked with numbers. "We're digging in grids nine and ten today," she explained. "Everyone choose a spot and shovel the dirt into these screens."

"I don't see why we have to dig here," Ellen said. "It's obvious there's something over there."

I looked where she pointed, but the ground appeared the same as our assigned patch.

Cecily gave her a hand shovel. "Let's see if you're right. You dig there first."

Stepping primly over the strings, Ellen swept her hand over the earth. Then she used the shovel to scoop out a hole about six inches deep.

"Not so fast," Cecily called, but before she could give further directions Ellen tossed aside the shovel and whipped out her brush.

"It's a huge bone," she announced. "Like from a dinosaur."

Despite Cecily's protests, we ran across the grid. The bone was yellow and crusted with dirt. I rested my hand on its rough surface, and my mind tingled with the amazing possibility of holding something from thousands of years ago.

Garrett, who was usually quiet, pushed his way to the front. "Let me feel it." The moment his fingers touched the bone, he shuddered. "This is an Apatosaurus bone. This dinosaur used to be called the brontosaurus. The bones are found in desert regions, so how'd it get here?"

"How'd you know that?" Ellen demanded. "I discovered it—I should have known it."

Cecily took the bone. "Eugene is going to bust a gasket missing this. You two have learned your gifts! Ellen, we call it dowsing when you can find buried objects. And Garrett, you're an empath. You know about things from touching them. Have either of you ever done this before?"

Ellen and Garrett stared at each other, their faces blank.

"Hmm, perhaps the air of Camp Hawthorne is working on both of you."

My head prickled in the heat. I wanted to touch the dinosaur bone again, but it turned blurry and seemed to be fading farther away. With this double vision, I couldn't claim the air of Camp Hawthorne was doing me any good. I sat down.

"You all right?" Lindsey's voice reached me faintly.

My mouth was dry, and when I looked at my hands they seemed to be doubling into twenty fingers. "I'm not sure..."

Cecily's face loomed over me. "Stella has heat stroke."

"I think I can find water," Ellen said, and then the light turned black.

Next thing I remember, a plastic bottle was being forced between my lips. "Quick, before it runs out."

The cool water splashed into my mouth, and I managed to swallow. Another gulp and then another, and then Cecily's face swam in front of me. "Any better?"

I tried to tell her I was fine, but my voice came out in a croak.

She peered at me. "The best we can do is get you down to Aunt Winnie's cabin. She'll be able to help."

Her image wavered, and everything went dark again.

CHAPTER FOURTEEN

I woke up in a dim room with bunches of dried flowers and leaves hanging over my head—the smell reminded me of the lavender Grandma put in her drawers. "Grandma?" I asked.

"No honey. It's Aunt Winnie here. You're staying with me till you feel better."

I followed the voice and saw a small woman in a wheelchair. Her skin was dark, but her hair was almost pure white. Her cheeks were so wrinkled she could have been the mother of my grandmother.

"My name's Stella," I said.

"Nice to meet you." Aunt Winnie wheeled herself closer and replaced the washcloth on my forehead with a new one. "You're wearing one of the old-time bandanas."

I felt my neck. The bandana was still there, but it was twisted to the side. "This was my mother's."

"Ah." Her eyes gleamed in the soft light.

"Both my parents were here—Franny and Dan. Did you ever meet them?"

Aunt Winnie lifted my wrist in her cool fingers. "Your pulse seems better." She peered into my face. "What happened up there?"

"We were at the dig, and Ellen found..."

"No, honey, when you got sick."

"The sun was hot, and everything went fuzzy and double."

"You see clearly now?"

I focused on the room—the quilt at the foot of the bed and the vases of wildflowers on the window sill, then nodded.

"Good," she said. "Now listen to me. If that double vision comes back, you close your eyes tight and concentrate on what you're really seeing."

Her words confused me, but there was something about the way she said them that made me think I needed to pay attention.

Someone knocked at the door, and Cecily's head appeared around it. "Is Stella ready to go back?"

Aunt Winnie patted my arm. "She's ready." She lowered her head and whispered to me, "Come visit, and I'll tell you what I can about your parents."

Her words drove away the last of my dizzy feeling, and I jumped up to follow Cecily. "I'll be back," I promised.

The rest of our group was waiting outside, muddy and jubilant. "Stella, look at all the stuff we found," Lindsey said.

Garrett waved the dinosaur bone, Jayden held up a handful of pottery pieces, Lindsey a clay pipe, and Freddy a tin box. Ellen stood off to the side, covered in dirt, but smiling.

"You should've seen Ellen," Lindsey continued. "When you fainted, she walked right up the hill and told us to dig, and we found a spring of water."

I should have been happy for Ellen, but something inside me shriveled. Everyone was finding their gifts. What if I didn't have one?

Lindsey linked her arm in mine as we walked back to camp. "You can get Ellen to help you find clues about your parents. Maybe they dropped something that's been buried in the sands of time."

I imagined the kids from my photograph dropping a soda can and a mound of dirt drifting over it, and I giggled. Lindsey always made me feel better.

Eugene took us to the evening program at the Whittier House. He shook his head over all the objects we'd found. "Twenty points for the Thornes," he crowed. "And you'll be in my dowsing class tomorrow," he said to Ellen.

Since Karen and I missed the dig, Ellen told us in detail how she'd seen each of the shards of pottery and the clay pipe in the ground. By the time she got to the bits of gravel mixed with the tin box, I was sick of the whole adventure.

I let my mind wander to Aunt Winnie and her invitation to visit again. I hugged to myself the thought that she might tell me something more about my parents.

The Whits lived off the right-turning path from the Junction Stone in a tidy white house with green shutters. It looked as old as ours, but more cheerful. Neatly-trimmed bushes lined the front of the house, and two baskets of marigolds bloomed on either side of the front steps.

Cecily led us to the parlor, a long room stretching from the front of the house to the back. With all the campers gathered, it was pretty snug, but we found a breezy spot near the back window. The host for the event was Thaisa, the girl's CIT at Whittier House. She was also the empathics teacher, as Cecily explained, which meant she could tell a story about any object she held.

Thaisa opened the evening by showing us a book that once belonged to John Greenleaf Whittier. She sat in a black rocking chair and swayed back and forth as she recited part of a poem called *Snowbound*. As she spoke in a low voice, I pictured the scene: a family gathered around the fire, a snow storm raging outside, and the strange guest. When she reached this part her voice swelled louder:

> *Another guest that winter night*
> *Flashed back from lustrous eyes the light.*
> *Unmarked by time, and yet not young,*
> *The honeyed music of her tongue*

"The poem's about real people," Cecily whispered. "The guest had gifts like us."

Though it was the middle of summer, I shivered. Thaisa ended the recitation with lines that repeated in my head long after:

> *"Sit with me by the homestead hearth,*
> *And stretch the hands of memory forth."*

After the reading, we divided into groups for tours of the house conducted by the Whits. We were in Thaisa's group, and she told us how Whittier was a Quaker who spoke out against slavery. "He was also sympathetic to those wrongly accused of witchcraft," she said. Her voice was so deep and mysterious that new goose bumps raised on my arms. "A Salem woman named Temperance Card was unjustly hanged, and Whittier wrote the inscription for her memorial, built two hundred years later."

Upstairs, Thaisa showed us a hole the author put in the door of his study so his pet bird could fly in and out. I thought I'd like a hole like that in my own room back home. Of course, I'd have to convince Grandma to let me have a bird, first.

Thaisa had a way of staring, as though she was looking straight through you. She stopped our group at the door before we left. "The Thornes are always welcome here," she said. "Nathaniel Hawthorne did a good turn for Whittier once."

"What does she mean?" Jayden muttered to Karen.

"There's a story called 'P's Correspondence'—Read it, and you'll understand."

Thaisa turned to Garrett. "I'll see you at the class for empathics tomorrow."

Freddy gave Garrett a soft punch. "Congratulations—you'll love the classes."

The magical feeling from the evening seemed to leak right out of me. Everyone else would be going to classes tomorrow, except me.

Chapter Fifteen

I woke up early the next day and made my way to the dining hall before anyone else was awake. A lot of things had happened, and I needed to think. I was surprised to find Jayden already there.

He was just pulling down a book from the shelf above the fireplace and grinned sheepishly when he saw me. "I just needed some time to read. I'm not used to being around people all the time."

Jayden was a different person at camp—more like the kid who used to pedal around the neighborhood with me, not the one who clammed up this past year. I hadn't realized how much I missed his friendship. I grabbed two slices of bread from the counter. "I know what you mean," I said. "Tell Cecily I'm going to skip breakfast this morning."

I followed the path to Aunt Winnie's place and ate the bread as I walked. The sun slanted through the trees, lighting up the specks of dust that floated in the air.

Aunt Winnie's cabin stood in the middle of a cluster of pine trees where the hill dipped into a hollow. She was in the yard, sitting in her wheelchair with a shallow bucket balanced on her knees. She made clucking noises as she sprinkled corn on the ground for the chickens, and they squawked and bobbed their heads to gulp the grains.

"Aren't chickens the most comical things?" Aunt Winnie said, as if we'd already been chatting for hours.

"Can I feed them?" I asked.

She passed me the bucket, and the chickens followed me around, pecking at my shoe when I let up for a moment. They were so interesting I almost forgot my reason for coming, but not for long. "Aunt Winnie, did you ever meet my parents?"

She tilted her head and studied me. "I did. Your mother made me this cord for my glasses. I was old even then, you know." She took off her glasses so I could touch the cord. "They call this stuff gimp."

The cord was made from the same plastic as my key chain, but the pattern was different—looser and more flexible. "Can you tell me more about them?"

Aunt Winnie looked out at the tree tops, as though she stored her memories up there. "Your mother arrived first, as I remember. She found her gift the first day—a gift for making intricate things with her fingers. She used to help me thread my needles, twenty at a time so I'd have one whenever I needed it."

Aunt Winnie's words flowed over me like a wind, setting everything right in my mind. I knew I'd never forget a single thing she said.

"Your father started coming the next year, and he was a handful." Aunt Winnie laughed, only it came out more like wheezing. "One day I woke up to find baby bonnets on all the piglets. He was in the telekinesis class with your mother, but he had another gift, too."

"Were they friends right away?"

"More like enemies. She thought he was a show-off. But by their fifth year they were counselors-in-training together, and something happened that made them friends."

"What was it?"

"It's a secret, honey," said Aunt Winnie, making her voice quiet. "But if you need to know, I promise I'll tell you by and by. For now it's safer this way."

Safer?

"Does my grandmother know?"

Aunt Winnie's face wrinkled. "No more questions for today."

≪⚜≫

Breakfast was just ending when I returned to the dining hall. Jayden jerked his head toward the door as he headed out to wash dishes, and I followed him. He got the dishes started in washing motion and leaned back against the brick wall. "I found that story Thaisa told us about," he said.

My mind was full of my meeting with Aunt Winnie. "Thaisa?" I muttered.

"Remember 'P's Correspondence?'"

I flushed. "Yes—Hawthorne's favor."

"The way Hawthorne tells it, there was a man who knew the alternate history of world events, and everyone

102

thought he was crazy. He mentions Whittier, but he only says he died young, which actually never happened."

"What does it mean?"

"If we told people what we know, they would say we were crazy, right?" He didn't wait for an answer. "What if Nathaniel Hawthorne wrote that story because it was a *real* alternate history? What if that's what Thaisa meant when she said Hawthorne did Whittier a good turn—he saved him from his alternate history?"

"Why don't you ask Thaisa?" I asked.

"For some reason they aren't telling us everything. Don't you think it's strange that we dug up a dinosaur bone yesterday that should have been in a desert? And why was Cecily so secretive about the scrap of paper you found? There's a mystery at the dig site—what if there's an alternate history going on there?"

I had a million objections to Jayden's theory, but the more I thought about it, the more I wondered if there might be some truth to it. "We'll have to keep our eyes and ears open if we want to find out more."

"Let's meet back here if we learn anything," he said.

When we were little, Jayden and I fixed a meeting place where all our adventures began. "It'll be like the tire swing at your house," I said.

"Our *new* meeting place." He grinned, and suddenly I felt a giddy happiness, like I was a kid again swinging through the air.

He left for class, and I watched him jog down the trail. Just as he disappeared, I remembered my talk with Aunt

Winnie and wondered if I should I have told him about it. Nothing seemed too important, except what she didn't tell me.

It was time for swim class, but I barely had a chance to dread it because Lindsey rushed up, skipping with excitement. "Cecily's teaching a craft workshop for people who haven't found their gift yet, and guess what we're learning?"

I tried to come up with things people did at regular camp. "Whittling?"

"Making stuff from gimp, like your mother's key chain."

My spirits lifted. "That's great—if I have to spend another morning learning to swim, I'll sink."

The craft class was held at our own Hawthorne House. Several girls from the other dorms came, along with Ivan from the Thornes. I suspect he only came to support Cecily. All the other guys chose swimming.

Cecily gave us long strands of any two colors we chose, and we sat on couches in the downstairs parlor. Despite the open window, the room kept its dismal air. The fireplace was made of dark red brick, and above the mantel the portrait of an old pilgrim glowered down at us.

Lindsey giggled. "He must be the source of all the gloom in this house."

"You can read about him in one of Hawthorne's books," Cecily said. "But I can tell you his story while we work."

It didn't take us long to learn how to weave the gimp. The first lesson was the box knot, and once we got it, we simply made it over and over.

While I twisted and wove the gimp, Cecily stood by the portrait. "Hawthorne wrote about this guy in a book called *The House of Seven Gables*, which was based on this house. This is the picture of Colonel Pyncheon from colonial days."

"Who was he?" asked Ivan. He was hopelessly tangled in his gimp, and he sat back to listen to the story.

"The founder of the family home." Cecily turned her back on the scowling portrait. "He accused a local carpenter of being a witch so he'd be executed and his land sold. As you can guess, the old colonel bought the property and built this house on it."

"Was the carpenter really a witch?" Lindsey asked.

Cecily's face darkened. "According to Hawthorne, the man set a dying curse on the old colonel, and it came true."

"What happened?" I asked.

"The family never found the deed to a huge amount of land they might have owned. The curse wasn't broken until several generations later when a descendent of the carpenter came to live here and fell in love with one of the colonel's descendents. Their love broke the curse, and they found the deed hidden behind this portrait."

Lindsey sighed. "I like happy endings."

My key chain was almost done, and Cecily showed me how to finish it off. I was still carrying my mother's key chain in my pocket, and I brought it out to show her.

"You should put it on a cord and wear it around your neck," she said. She pulled off a length of shiny blue gimp to match the key chain and slipped it through the loop on the end. "It shows you're a legacy."

"What's a legacy?"

"That's what we call campers whose parents came to Camp Hawthorne."

I remembered Cecily told us her mother came here.

"To hear my mother talk about this place, you'd suppose it was the most amazing place in creation."

I thought it probably was. I slipped the key chain under my T-shirt. It felt good to have it close.

After class we helped wind the gimp on spools. "Cecily, why aren't you teaching a real class?" I asked.

She blushed. "Mine doesn't meet during the day."

"What's your gift?"

"Ah, sort of talking."

Talking—that made sense. She was a really strong talker.

"To animals, I mean. It sometimes works on people."

"Animals?" Lindsey said. "That's fantastic."

"Well, it's more like being able to transmit and receive impressions."

Ivan perked up at the mention of animals. "Have you ever talked with farm animals? My family keeps dairy cows, and I've always wanted to know what they're thinking."

Cecily laughed. "Cows are pretty dense. They mostly think of grass."

"That explains a lot," Ivan said.

CHAPTER SIXTEEN

Ivan raved to everyone at lunch about Cecily's gift. "Imagine—with a gift like that you could talk to horses. Horses!"

Coop grew pale during this talk. He'd been at the lake all morning, and I wondered if he had a touch of heat stroke, but after lunch he edged up next to Cecily while we were washing the dishes out back.

"I can talk with chickens," he said, his voice so soft we almost didn't hear him.

Cecily was kneeling over a bin of soapy water, but she sat back on her heels. "Chickens?"

"Yeah, could it be—you know—a gift?"

I was almost glad I hadn't found my gift yet. It was killing Coop to talk about it.

"Well, I don't see why not," Cecily said, bounding up and shaking him by the hand. "Glad to know you, Coop. It's been a long time since a new animal-talker joined us. The others will be thrilled." She reeled off the names of half a dozen campers from other dorms. "We're having our craft class tonight at the fire ring by the lake. You'll be surprised at all the critters that jabber away at night."

I left them discussing the interesting wildlife at Camp Hawthorne. It was getting harder and harder to believe I had a gift.

I returned to the dining hall and found Lindsey standing in front of the point chart.

"We have a robotics competition this afternoon," she said. "Eugene says we need a solid win to catch the Fellows." She paused and studied me. "Stella, have you noticed you aren't taking those deep breaths as much?"

I took an experimental breath, and it was true. I didn't feel the need to fill my lungs and hold it every few minutes like I did last school year. "Cecily said the air of this place works on people. Do you think the air really makes a difference, or was it just one of her expressions?"

"I don't know. Ellen didn't believe anything at first, and now look at her."

"Jayden, too." We were silent a moment.

"Stella, promise me one thing—you won't feel bad if I find my gift."

"Of course I won't." Inside, however, I was groaning. Lindsey probably knew her gift already and didn't want to hurt my feelings.

Jayden, carrying a long thin case, joined us at the board. When he saw me looking at it, he held it out. "It's a flute case. All the telekinetics learn an instrument."

"Karen plays the bugle, doesn't she?" I asked.

"And the drums."

That explained our wake-up call the first day.

We walked together to the Twain House for the robot competition. I hadn't been inside the house yet, and it was as fancy inside as it was outside. The front door opened to a deep foyer with stairs whose carved railings spiraled up to the second floor. The ceiling was painted red with intricate designs of black and silver.

All the teams were gathered in the library, and we found the Thornes at the far end, where green light filtered through the plants in a glass alcove.

Ivan rushed up to us. "Where's Eugene?" he asked.

"He's checking out the dig site again," Jayden said. He glanced at me, eyebrows raised, and I knew he thought something important was going on.

Cecily clapped her hands. She waited for Joanne and her friends to settle down, while the rest of us sat on the floor around her. "All right, Thornes. Today is the annual robotics competition. Camp Hawthorne has a long legacy of inventors, and some of the things they made are still secret."

Ivan was having a hard time sitting still, and I noticed his arms were covered in spots. "What happened to your arms?" I whispered to him.

He looked down and jumped straight into the air. "It's spreading!" he cried. He tore off his shirt, and I saw red bumps scattered thickly over his back and chest.

"It's chicken pox." Cecily's voice cut through the surprised chatter. "You need to show Mr. Parker."

Lindsey offered to go with him since she'd had chicken pox already. Ivan stared at his arms in disbelief as she shepherded him toward the door.

After his departure, Cecily explained how we would build our robot on the base from last year, but most of it didn't make sense. She divided us into squads, and I hoped the others would know what to do. Jayden and Freddy were in my group.

Our squad leader was named Roderick. He wore thick glasses and squinted at us. "Our task is to make an arm to sweep up objects," he announced. "We'll add a pressure sensor for walls."

I didn't understand a word he said, but Freddy started sifting through the bin of structural pieces. "Would this work?" he asked, holding up a bar of metal with holes cut in it every couple inches.

Roderick inspected it. "Needs to be longer."

Jayden found more bars and a handful of nuts and bolts. "We can connect three bars together to make a longer arm," he said.

Once he started putting them together, I saw what he was doing. "What if it worked on a hinge?" I asked. "We could loosen the bolt on this piece so it would bend."

"Brilliant," Roderick said. "Now, we need to add a scoop on the end."

I went back to the bin for parts, but Ellen was there with her arms buried up to the elbows. "I'm seeing if I can use my gift to find pieces buried in a pile," she said. "Tell me what you need."

I secretly hoped it wouldn't work. "We need something broad like a scoop."

"Is that all? Here."

She handed me the perfect piece, and she didn't even smirk.

"Thanks," I said. I couldn't figure Ellen out.

Jayden fastened the scoop to the end, and Roderick added the pressure sensor. I had to admit it looked pretty good. We dubbed it the "super sweeper" and took it to Cecily. I felt proud when she admired the hinge effect.

We hung around while she snapped our super sweeper onto the main robot. "Are there a lot of people with ESP who are good at stuff like this?" Freddy asked.

"Sure, Thomas Edison was one of us. He was a friend of Twain and did one of his earliest film experiments in this house."

"Really?" said Freddy, his ginger eyebrows shooting up. "Buckeye assigned us one of Twain's books today. I thought it'd be about Tom Sawyer and Huck Finn, but it was totally different. It was about a guy who time-traveled to the middle ages and set himself up as a wizard because he had all kinds of modern know-how."

I thought Lindsey would like to hear about that book. Ever since Freddy brought up time-travel on our hike, she insisted it would be the next great invention—her idea of super-advanced science. But Lindsey didn't return until the squads had finished their parts and Cecily had added them to the robot.

We were starting the first test run on the competition board when Lindsey squeezed in next to me.

"Where have you been?" I asked. "Was Ivan worse than we thought?"

"No, I just helped Mr. Parker bring his clothes from Hawthorne House. He's going to bunk here so Buckeye can keep an eye on him."

The robot whirred to life and began its slow progression, but Lindsey stared beyond it to the glass alcove where the green leaves shimmered in the afternoon sun. "Stella, I talked with Mr. Parker and told him about my gift."

"What? You found your gift?"

"I've known for a while. I can transfer thought."

"Like reading minds?"

"Sort of, but it has to be a willing communicator."

That gave me a creepy feeling. "Have you been reading my mind all this time?"

Lindsey smiled at me. "Of course—we're best friends, after all. You even caught some of my thinking, didn't you?"

She was right.

I hardly paid attention after that to the competition. In a daze I watched our robot face off against the various teams. I only realized the tournament was over when the Twains began jumping up and down, signaling their victory.

We walked to the dining hall for dinner, and I asked Lindsey if I needed to talk anymore since she could just transfer brain waves around. She laughed at me. "We'll always need to talk, Stella." She told me she would begin craft classes with Mr. Parker's group tomorrow. I imagined I'd be the only one left swimming in the lake.

∽∾

We had a campfire that evening. I sat with the other Thornes and watched the gray smoke rising into the dusk. I hoped Grandma was all right back home. I'd written to tell her about our robot, but we weren't allowed to tell our families about the ESP part of camp, unless they already knew about it, like Cecily's family. It felt strange keeping a secret from Grandma.

After we sang the camp song, Mr. Parker greeted everyone. "We've had an exciting day with our robot competition." He paused while the Twains burst into cheers. "And Eugene reports that we found some important artifacts at the dig today." The Thornes let out whoops for him.

"They found a colonial shoe buckle," Jayden told us in an undertone.

"Shush, we're supposed to keep it secret," Cecily said.

Jayden looked at me, and I knew he was thinking about "P's Correspondence." Could there be a connection—our dig site somehow mixed up with an alternate history? I shook my head. A colonial shoe buckle didn't prove anything.

Mr. Parker continued, "And now for another one of our Camp Hawthorne traditions—campfire stories." He introduced a CIT from Longfellow House named Vangie,

114

who began the evening with a poem by Longfellow. It was one of those quiet poems that made me stare at the fire and think. Her words kept rolling over and over again in my head—*Not enjoyment, and not sorrow, is our destined end or way; but to act, that each to-morrow find us farther than to-day.* Mr. Parker let everyone reflect quietly for a while.

Next, Eugene came forward and told a whopping ghost story about a proud beauty named Alice. In a hollow voice he recounted how she spurned the love of a poor carpenter, who used his strange powers to hypnotize her until she went insane and died. "And her ghost haunted the house ever after," he concluded, his low voice sending prickles across my scalp.

"That's one of the family curses I told you about this morning," Cecily whispered.

Lindsey squeaked. "I'm not going to sleep all night."

We finished the evening with s'mores. I felt like an old pro, spearing my marshmallow and crisping it over the fire. With the blaze of stars overhead and the gentle crackling of the fire, a feeling of calm washed over me. I pushed my worries about my gift way back in my mind and instead thought about my parents and how they probably ate s'mores just like this. I imagined my mother threading needles for Aunt Winnie and my dad hatching his pranks. I let the gooey chocolate melt in my mouth. Tomorrow I would find out more.

CHAPTER SEVENTEEN

The next morning I snuck away again to Aunt Winnie's cabin before anyone else woke up. The sun was just rising, but Aunt Winnie was already wheeling around her yard, feeding the chickens.

"Thought I might see you today," she said, as she handed me the bucket of corn.

I told her about Lindsey finding her gift. "And now I'm the last one in Hawthorne House who doesn't know what they can do. Except for Ivan, but he has chicken pox. What if I don't have a gift at all?"

A chicken fluttered to Aunt Winnie's lap, and she stroked it slowly. "Seems to me you're always rushing around trying to find out stuff—about your parents and your gift. Have you ever stopped to consider there might be a reason you aren't finding things?" She looked up at the pines whispering in the morning breeze and paused as though listening to them. "Let me tell you a story, child. Come here and sit on this bench."

A lump was rising in my throat, but I sat next to her.

"A long time ago, my people lived in the deep south. They were slaves and didn't even know it, until a man named John Greenleaf Whittier came to town. He said no one had a right to own another person, and the moment he said it, we knew he was right. My great-grandfather was only a boy, but he wanted to run away that night. He had a friend on the plantation—a girl—and she could see what might happen. What might happen, you understand?"

I didn't really understand, but I nodded.

"Eudora was her name, and she saw that if he ran away first thing, there would be trouble. But if he waited, there might be a way. Well, Mr. Whittier went back home, but he didn't forget the people down south, and one night a friend of his visited the plantation and told my people he had a plan to smuggle them away north, where they could live free. Eudora looked in the future, and she knew it would work, but she also knew she had to stay behind." Aunt Winnie stopped and searched my face. I squirmed because I knew she was trying to tell me something, but it didn't make sense.

"What happened?"

Her eyes stared into mine for another moment.

"My great-grandfather and his family got away, and Mr. Whittier brought them to live on this land. A few years later, the Civil War came along, and all the slaves went free. My great-grandfather went back, and he found Eudora. She'd grown into a beautiful woman by then, and they got married and raised their family in this very cabin."

"So, Eudora was your great-grandmother?"

"She was—and she had a rare gift. The same one Mr. Hawthorne had—the gift that helped him write all those stories. He could see what might happen."

I thought of Jayden and his ideas about "P's Correspondence." "Can people with this gift change what will happen?"

"Knowledge always changes things."

I was afraid to ask the next question, but I had to know. "Aunt Winnie, do you have this gift?"

"I do, and it tells me it's dangerous for you to keep looking for stories about your parents. You understand?"

I tried to swallow, but the lump in my throat got stuck.

Back at the dining hall, I spotted Jayden and motioned for him to follow me out back. "You were right about Hawthorne," I said as he dumped the plates in a bin. "He saved Whittier because he knew what might happen."

I told him everything Aunt Winnie said, and Jayden listened so hard he forgot to set the dishes washing. "What did she mean about *knowledge changing things*?" he asked. "Is there a connection with our dig site? And why did she say it was dangerous to learn about your parents?"

"I'm not sure, but I've been getting warning notes about them."

Jayden's eyes narrowed. "Do you still have them?"

The last note was in my pocket, and Jayden studied it for a long time before handing it back to me. "Your parents must be involved," he concluded.

We talked the whole way to our next class about the possibilities. Even though Aunt Winnie said it was dangerous, we were determined to learn more.

"I'm glad we're friends again," I told him.

"We've always been friends."

"Even though you didn't talk the whole last year?"

He thrust out his chin, and I worried I'd sent him back inside himself, but he kept on talking. "When I was a kid I believed everything Grandma Charlotte said—how I could be anything I wanted to be. But I guess at some point I lost hope."

"Is that when you started reading all the time?"

"Yeah. When I read, I escaped and got back some of those dreams." He grew silent for a few paces before he spoke again. "Camp has taught me there are more things in this world than I ever imagined."

I was glad for Jayden. He had a gift, but where did that leave me?

We split up at the campfire circle. His telekinesis class was meeting there. I had swimming, but I was so caught up in my talk with Jayden, I forgot to dread it.

When I arrived, the others had just decided to quit. There were only three of us left, and the girl from the Whits told me she had a feeling her gift would appear today, anyway. I wished I had a feeling like that, but I only had Aunt Winnie's voice playing in my head: "You run after things too much."

Since I didn't have to swim, I watched Jayden's class for a while. They were moving the logs around the campfire circle. Karen barely made the logs wobble, but Jayden actually lifted them off the ground.

Skeeter gave them a break, and Karen and Jayden came over to me. "Aren't you swimming today?" he asked.

"No, I thought I'd visit Ivan." I was embarrassed to admit I had nothing to do.

Jayden levitated his backpack toward us. "I have a book for him."

Skeeter blew the whistle for class to start again, and I headed back up the path to Twain House. At least I could talk with my one remaining friend who hadn't found his gift.

I found Ivan in Buckeye's room. Vangie, the Fellow's CIT, was bringing him his meal and said I could visit for a few minutes. She passed the tray to him, and he sighed.

"You okay?" I asked, pulling a chair next to his bed.

"Not really." He started itching a patch of red welts on his arm, and Vangie picked up a pink bottle and advanced on him. "No more calamine lotion—I'll stop," he yelped.

"Is it that bad?" I tried to sound sympathetic, but Ivan's grimaces made me laugh.

"It's not that. I ran a fever last night and accidentally discovered my gift." His eyes slid sideways to a pile of sodden sheets in the corner. Charred patches showed where fire had burned spots. "I could've had the gift of talking with horses, but no—I got fire," he said.

"Fire?"

"I can summon it like this." He held up a finger with a flame on the tip.

"Not while you're sick," Vangie said. "Time for your guest to leave so you can rest."

I propped the book beside his pillow. "Jayden thought you'd like to read Hawthorne's *Wonder Book*. It'll help pass the time."

Other friends must have visited already, because *Tom Sawyer* and *The Song of Hiawatha* lay on his bedside table.

"Thanks," Ivan said. "These stories might give me ideas for what I can do with fire."

I left him gloomily picking at his food and muttering, "It could have been horses."

ॐ

The evening program was a band performance at the Alcott House. It was the smallest of the dorms, a yellowish green house sitting at the foot of a steep hill. The musicians would perform in the barn, and the Thornes had the job of setting up chairs. Cecily directed operations in between bursts of information about Alcott House.

"This is a copy of the house where Louisa May Alcott lived as a young teen," she said, handing me two folding chairs. "She wrote *Little Women* about her life here."

Lindsey clutched my arm. "That's one of my favorite books!"

"Mine, too," Cecily said. "Louisa used to put on plays for her family and neighbors in this barn."

Lindsey forgot to unfold her chairs and stood staring at the four walls. "Jo was here," she murmured.

I took the chairs from her and set them on the end of the row as Cecily chattered on. "Later, Hawthorne bought this house from the Alcotts, and they moved to a house next door."

"They were neighbors?" Lindsey squeaked.

I finished the row while she spouted questions about the main house—were there stairs for playing pilgrims? Was there a garret? I suspected she wouldn't be paying much attention to the concert.

The band members arrived, and most of them were telekinetics like Jayden, though there were a few campers who studied instruments year round. They stood out from the others because they rustled their sheet music in a determined way, while the telekinetics joked and nudged each other. Some telekinetics didn't even have sheet music.

Karen slouched in and stationed herself beside Joanne, whose oboe rose in the air and began trilling on its own. Joanne grabbed it and shot her a poisonous look. Karen pretended to busy herself polishing her bugle.

While we waited for the concert to begin, Lindsey told us about her first day of class. "He puts us in pairs, and we send messages to each other. Today we shared our favorite color and ice cream. My partner and I didn't get it at first, but then we figured out we were blocking each other. After that we made great progress. We even learned how to share information with a large group."

"How do you do it?"

"If one person provides information, I can send it to everyone else."

"Sounds boring," Ellen said. "Our class is much better. Eugene has us hiking around camp looking for buried stuff. We find mostly trash, like soda bottles, but today I found this." She pulled out a grimy key chain like the ones we made with Cecily.

"One of the empaths might know who it belonged to," I said, then immediately wished I hadn't. Ellen loved being the center of attention, and this key chain was her ticket to going around and showing off what she found.

Freddy and some of the guys arrived and took seats near us.

"Hey Garrett," Ellen said. "I wondered if you could tell me who dropped this."

He smiled shyly and took the key chain, weighing it in his palm. He stiffened. "Weird."

"What's weird?" she asked.

"This key chain is three hundred years old."

"Impossible—plastic wasn't even invented then."

He handed it back as though it burned him. "It's true though. It's from Colonial times."

The band started up a thundering version of *The Star Spangled Banner*, and everyone stood to sing. As I sang, I looked at Garrett. Was he making a joke? He caught my eye and nodded. What was he trying to say?

CHAPTER EIGHTEEN

I didn't sleep well that night. Every time I woke up, my mind returned to the key chain and Aunt Winnie and my parents. Finally I got up as the windows turned a lighter gray and made my way to the dining hall.

I sat on the front porch with my arms clasped around my knees to keep out the morning chill and watched the sun break over the pine trees. I hadn't been there long when the door of Twain House opened and closed with a sigh, and a shadowy form walked toward me. It was Buckeye in his safari hat and blue bandana.

"Lovely morning," he said, sitting beside me.

I didn't say anything.

"I don't sleep well, myself," he explained. "Too many regrets."

"It's not that for me. I hoped being here would help me learn about my parents."

The sun had risen higher and cast a pinkish glow around us. Buckeye turned to me, and for once his shiny smile was gone. "Stella, there are some things we can never find out, no matter how hard we try. Perhaps you need to accept this."

I put my head on my knees and let the tears trickle down my cheeks. Buckeye was right, but I didn't want to let go. I felt a pat on my shoulder and heard the door to the dining hall swing as Buckeye headed inside.

Though Aunt Winnie didn't want me asking about my parents, I needed a visit this morning. Just talking with someone who knew them gave me a connection—like I was holding onto a rope with my parents at the other end. Besides, I had plenty of other things to ask her.

Aunt Winnie was in her cabin, wheeling back and forth as she poured water in the pots of flowers that filled every table top and window sill.

She shook her head when I told her about Ellen's key chain and what Garrett said. "Trouble never seems to leave Camp Hawthorne," she muttered.

"What do you mean?"

She peered into my face. "You realize your gift yet? Hmm. I wonder." She emptied the pitcher and began drying it. "You have a gift for attracting question marks."

I laughed. "Is that a real gift?"

"No, it's a curse," said Aunt Winnie. "Reminds me of that fella, Thomas Edison."

She parked her wheelchair next to the couch, and I sat by her. "Stella, you know a lot of people with ESP invent things. It sort of runs in their blood."

I thought of the robot competition. "I've seen some of it."

"When Mark Twain helped start the camp, he brought his friend Thomas Edison, and they built something here.

It was lost, but some people think it turned up again around the time your parents came. Odd things happened in those days, and strange stuff appeared at the dig site." Aunt Winnie gazed at me through her glasses. "Now do you understand how Garrett might be telling the truth?"

"Not exactly." Aunt Winnie's words made my hands prickle.

"You will," she said. "Better get going before they start searching for you." Aunt Winnie seemed to sag in her chair. I squeezed her hand, but she didn't look up. I hoped I hadn't made more trouble by coming here.

Breakfast was ending and everyone was rushing out of the dining hall when I returned. I wanted to tell Jayden what I'd learned from Aunt Winnie, but I couldn't find him anywhere. I hoped he'd know what she meant about Garrett. How could he be telling the truth about the key chain? I wanted to ponder this idea more, but Vangie marched up and put a tray in my hands. "Could you take this to Ivan?" It was more of a command than a request.

I walked in to find Ivan clutching his arms in agony. "Calamine lotion," he said, through gritted teeth. His arms were covered in small burn marks.

"You haven't been using fire on those chicken pox?" I asked.

"Calamine lotion," he gasped. "In the closet."

I opened the door and saw a dozen of Buckeye's khaki shirts hanging on the rod.

"Shelf in back," Ivan said.

Pushing aside the shirts, I uncovered a shelf filled with boxes and bottles. The pink bottle stood next to a pair of shoes. I reached around them, but something about their color and shape caught my eye. They were brown with square toes. I jumped back and hit my head on the closet rod, and for a moment everything became fuzzy.

My voice seemed to come from a long way off. "Ivan, what are these shoes doing here?"

"Calamine," he repeated, as if it was his dying word.

My vision returned to normal, and I rushed the lotion to him. Ivan began slapping it over both arms, grunting with relief. "Sorry, Stella. I tried an experiment that didn't work. Don't tell Vangie, okay?"

"Of course I won't, but those brown shoes in the closet—do they belong to you?"

"No, my stuff's in this bag. She only keeps the extra medicine there."

I didn't want to burden Ivan with my worries, but was Buckeye one of the brown people? Could he be the one sending the warning notes?

I needed to find Mr. Parker, but he wasn't in his office. I ran out of Twain House, right into a crowd of people. Three camp buses sat in the long driveway, and Buckeye was waving his clipboard and herding campers into them.

I shrank back and bumped into Cecily.

"We're supposed to wait in the dining hall," she told me. "Hawthorne House is going last."

"Have you seen Mr. Parker?" I asked.

"He already left on the first bus."

I tried to quiet my swirling thoughts as we walked across the driveway. I would talk with Mr. Parker when we arrived at the field trip.

"How's Ivan?" Cecily asked.

"Gloomy as ever. But he's fixed up with calamine lotion for a while."

"He'll probably flip his lid over missing this field trip," she said.

"Where are we going?"

Cecily shrugged. "Buckeye didn't say, but we usually go to the seashore. You should've seen what Eugene's group dug up last year—six pirate doubloons and an old wine bottle from the Titanic."

We found the others from Hawthorne House already seated around tables. Jayden was reading a book, and I slipped into the chair next to him. "I talked with Aunt Winnie again," I whispered.

His eyes brightened. "Any clues to our mystery?"

"I'm not sure. She told me Thomas Edison came here and made something with Twain that might explain the odd stuff at the dig site, and how Garrett spoke the truth about the key chain."

He flipped to a page with a bookmark. "I'm reading 'P's Correspondence' again to see if I can find a clue."

The other kids were sitting at tables playing cards, and Eugene called across the room to Ellen. "Garrett says he's right about that key chain you showed him, and he wants to prove it to you."

She bounced up. "I wouldn't have bothered about this silly old thing, but since you really want to show us."

We gathered around as she brought out the key chain, which she wore on a cord around her neck. I felt for my own key chain on its matching cord. It made me mad that Ellen had to mimic even this special link with my parents.

Garrett took the key chain and held it in his open palm. It seemed to tremble there, and I rubbed my eyes. They were acting up. I looked again and everything came back in focus.

"This key chain belonged to a girl named Hepzibah," he said. I startled at the name and glanced at Jayden, who nodded and tapped the book in his hand.

"She was afraid," Garrett continued. "Someone accused her of being a witch, and other people were dying. It was Salem, 1693."

Ellen made a movement to take back the key chain, but Garrett held it higher and his words came faster. "She got it from a girl named Franny, who made it at Camp Hawthorne."

My breath caught in my throat. This was the link between my parents and the mystery!

"Franny visited Salem and went away, and Hepzibah buried the key chain in her garden. No one ever found it until Ellen dug it up," Garrett said.

"What are you lot up to?"

We jumped guiltily. Buckeye stood in the doorway with his clipboard. "We've filled the buses, and I'll be sending one back for you," he said. "Make sure you're wearing comfortable shoes." He winked and left us.

I'd barely heard his words.

Ellen snatched the key chain and dangled it from her hand. "I've found something huge."

"It could be evidence of time travel," Eugene said. "But that's not an ESP gift I've ever heard of."

"It must be," said Ellen. "This Franny is the key to the whole thing."

I couldn't stand it. "Franny was my mother," I said.

Ellen spun to look at me. "It might be a different Franny."

I pulled out my key chain—a perfect match. "She made this when she came here."

"We could ask her then," she said, frowning.

"She died when I was a baby." I choked on the last words and the entire room grew silent. Lindsey wrapped an arm around me and led me from the circle.

"I didn't know," Ellen said. "No one ever told me."

Tears rolled down my face, and I couldn't stop them. I didn't want everyone to see me crying, so I headed for the door. Lindsey followed right behind me.

఼ఴఴ

CHAPTER NINETEEN

఼ఴఴ

I ran down the trail to the lake. Roots tripped my feet and Lindsey called for me to wait, but I couldn't stop. Stumbling past the shore and up into the hills toward Aunt Winnie's cabin, I tried to outrun my misery and all my questions about my parents.

Lindsey finally caught up with me, and a quiet thought invaded my mind.

Why are we going here?

"Aunt Winnie might have the answers," I said aloud.

We jogged the rest of the way in silence, but when we reached the cabin I groaned. The chicken house lay splintered in the yard, and the cabin door was smashed. Only a piece of it swung crazily on one hinge.

"Aunt Winnie," I yelled, darting inside. The bed was pulled apart—quilts lying on the floor and the mattress ripped. Every vase and pot was shattered and the flowers crushed. "Where's Aunt Winnie?" I cried.

Lindsey stood completely still, a strange look on her face. "Something's wrong with the others. We've got to go back."

"But, we have to find Aunt Winnie first."

"She's not here, Stella. The others need us more."

I couldn't imagine anything more urgent than Aunt Winnie gone and her cabin torn apart. Who would do that? Aunt Winnie was too frail. She couldn't survive an attack like this. I was caught in a mudslide of emotions, and all I could do was run back to where I started.

We ran so fast that my side ached and my vision was blurring. We entered the dining hall, and I closed my eyes to steady myself. I heard Eugene's voice bellowing above the din of people talking. "Everyone calm down and take a seat!"

Lindsey pulled me to a table. I opened my eyes, and Eugene came into clear view.

"This note came through the window," he said. "We don't know if it's reliable or some sort of prank." He handed it to Garret. "Can you tell who wrote it?"

Garrett touched the paper. "Buckeye," he said.

Everyone started talking again, but Cecily's voice cut through the clamor. "Read it again, Eugene. Slowly this time."

Eugene took the note and read:

> **This is a ransom note. If you want to see the other campers and staff unharmed, send Stella Harski to the lab. She may bring two people with her. You will find three pairs of shoes in the room with Ivan to transport you. Come at once.**

Cecily whispered to Eugene, and his jaw clenched. She held up a hand. "Y'all know we take precautions at Camp Hawthorne—no cell phones or electronic devices. That's because there are dangerous people who would take advantage of our gifts for their own ends." She looked at Eugene, and he nodded for her to continue. "There've been indicators that something big is about to happen. Some of our best practitioners have disappeared, and no one knows who is behind it. We suspect this kidnapping is part of it."

"But why Stella?" Jayden asked.

I was wondering the same thing. Was it because I was the only one without a gift? But then, why allow me to bring the others? I shrank into my chair, still out of breath from running.

Eugene growled, "We can't follow the directions. It's too dangerous."

"Isn't there someone we could ask for help?" Karen asked. "Maybe Aunt Winnie…"

"She's gone," Lindsey said. "And her cabin's torn apart."

Everyone was quiet for a moment as the gravity of the situation sank in.

"How about our parents?" Coop said.

Eugene crumpled the ransom note. "Where would we tell them to come?"

"There must be some authority we can contact," Ellen said.

Everyone stared at each other, their faces blank. "Only Mr. Parker would have known that," said Eugene.

How could we stand up to someone who kidnapped four busloads of kids? I thought about Camp Hawthorne and the wonderful world I'd discovered here. I'd do anything to protect it. My vision wobbled, and something clicked in my brain. "I need to go," I said.

Ellen squinted at me.

"I'll go," said Jayden.

"Me, too," said Lindsey.

"And me," said Ellen.

I forgot for a moment how miserable everything was. It felt good to know I had friends who would stick by me, no matter what.

Freddy stepped forward. "I don't mean to be pushy, but I should go, too. If I can read hidden writing, it might help us."

"Wait," Karen said. "What if it's a trap?"

"They have everyone else," I said. "Three more people won't make a difference. If we don't come back, the rest of you will have to rescue us."

I looked at Jayden and Ellen. "Thanks for volunteering to come with me, but I'll need the gifts Lindsey and Freddy have."

I thought they might argue, but Jayden nodded slowly. "I'll watch the shoe transport."

Eugene, Cecily and Ellen came as well. We walked across the driveway, and Jayden stayed at my side. "They might want you because of the connection with your parents," he said. "Be careful."

Ellen yanked open the door to Ivan's room. He was reading a book in bed while balancing a tray of cookies on his knee. He jumped, and the cookies flew in the air, landing in a shower of crumbs on his bedspread.

"What's going on?" he yelped.

"We're here for shoes," Ellen said.

I opened the cupboard and pushed back Buckeye's shirts. At the end of the row hung a single white lab coat with a picture I.D.

"It's Buckeye," I said. "But the name on the tag says Bradford Jaeger."

"You didn't think his real name was Buckeye, did you?" Ellen asked.

"No." It was hard to sort it all out. "But everything about him has been a lie."

"We know that," Ellen snapped. "That's why we're searching for shoes."

I turned back to the cupboard and scanned the shelf of medicine bottles. The first pair of brown shoes was still there, and near the bottom were two more pairs.

"We need to figure out how they work," I said.

"No time," said Freddy, jamming his feet into the largest pair. A low buzzing sounded, and he disappeared.

Lindsey clutched my shoulder. "What just happened?"

"See if you can reach his mind," I said.

She let her arms go loose and closed her eyes. "He's surprised, but no harm."

I held my breath and slipped on the second pair. They were a little big, but the instant my feet settled in the shoes, the air hummed and a sharp tug pulled under my rib cage.

Ivan's room zipped away, and I found myself standing with Freddy in a completely white office—white chairs, white carpet and a white table—with a communicating window in one wall. On the table lay a collection of newspapers. Freddy leaned over them scanning for information.

Lindsey arrived next to me, still bent in position to put on her shoes. "Where are we?"

"It must be the kidnapper's lab," I began, but a rattling at the window stopped me.

A tall woman with hair like a beehive slid the glass aside. "Stella Harski? You may come through."

A section of wall opened, and she led us to a door at the end of the passage, where she punched numbers on a keypad. We entered, and the door clanged shut.

This room was also white, but the light was even brighter. I squinted at a dozen tables ringing the room, each with its own pulsing box of light above it. In the center stood a giant machine made of reflective metal. The only blotch of color in the room was our hazy reflection—three kids in jeans and T-shirts.

A man, wearing a white lab coat and safety glasses, stepped from behind the contraption. He was barely taller than me, and if his hair hadn't been gray, I might have mistaken him for a kid. He put down a wrench and paused to study us. Lindsey flinched, and then I felt it, too—a gentle probing in my mind.

No, I thought with all the intensity I could muster.

"You did well to follow my instructions." His voice was mild, almost welcoming. "My name is Dr. Card, and I'm the president of a humanitarian organization called the Human Project."

"That kidnaps people," I blurted.

"For the good of humanity." He smiled—his teeth perfectly straight and bright white. "Those shoes, for example. We developed them in our lab. They can transport people anywhere in the world. Instantly. So you see, we are improving transportation for everyone."

"Then why haven't we heard of them?"

"A matter of economics, my dear. The shoes give a financial advantage that I will use to further the welfare of humanity, especially for people like us. Do you understand?"

I scowled. I had to concentrate to keep his soothing words from making me relax.

He walked over to a table crowded with shiny metal instruments. "You might be interested to know that many alumni of Camp Hawthorne work in my labs, once they understand the benefit to themselves."

I didn't like the way he said *benefit*. Was it the same kind of *benefit* he used to get us here—threats of harming our friends?

"Our organization spans the world now," he continued. "We have laboratories in almost every civilized nation, and some uncivilized ones as well. Our scientists work day and night to develop the tools we need to change the world."

"I saw the newspapers in the waiting room," Freddy said.

"Yes. Those skirmishes in Africa were us. We ended them, too."

"Why start things if you're only going to end them?" I asked.

His eyes narrowed. "That is not the point of our discussion. I brought you here because our lab needs a machine that was lost years ago. Our experts learned it is hidden at Hawthorne House, and Miss Harski will find it. You will know it by this marker."

He held up a card with the figure of a red triangle inside a black square. It looked familiar, but I couldn't remember where I'd seen it before.

"For now your friends believe they are on a harmless field trip with their leader Buckeye. But if you don't bring me the machine this evening, things will be very different."

Freddy was staring at the lab table piled with notes.

I felt Lindsey tremble slightly beside me. "We should get back to camp," I said as she swayed against me. Her body went limp, and I caught her before she hit the ground. "Now," I added, trying to keep my voice from shaking.

Dr. Card turned back to his contraption. "Just concentrate on where you want to go, and the shoes will take you there. You will get further instructions when the time comes."

"Camp Hawthorne," I said, the words feeling stiff in my mouth. The shoes buzzed and glowed, and a moment later we were back in Ivan's room.

CHAPTER TWENTY

Ivan shrieked, and a spurt of fire shot from his fingers.

Freddy helped Lindsey sit in a chair, and her eyes fluttered open. "What happened?"

"You began to shake when you were staring at Dr. Card," I said.

She rubbed her eyes. "I thought I could get inside his head and find out more. He let me in, but it was like standing on a cliff and looking down at the whole world. Vast power. He wanted us to know that."

Freddy shook his head. "I had the same impression from the newspapers in the waiting room. I got a clue, though. The lab papers mentioned something called the Pandora Device."

"What is it?" I asked.

"Didn't say."

Jayden tapped *The Wonder Book* by Ivan's bed. "Hawthorne wrote a bunch of stories for kids, and there's one called Pandora's Box—about a girl who was supposed to guard a secret trunk. She wanted to know what was inside so badly that she opened it, and all the troubles of the world came out."

I groaned. That sounded like a box Dr. Card would like. "His lab predicted I'd find the device, and he wants it."

"So what do we do?" Ellen cut in. "Let this monster control us?"

I realized how nice it was to have her on my side for once. Her anger made me feel stronger somehow.

"No," I said. "We find the machine first. Then *we* control what happens."

Eugene exchanged a triumphant glance with Cecily. "We might know where it is."

"Where?" several voices asked, but Cecily just shook her head. "We have to show you."

Ivan insisted on coming with us, and we picked up the rest of the Thornes at the dining hall. Cecily kept urging us to walk faster. "Y'all are slow as Christmas coming!" she said.

At the house, she took us to the dining room and opened a narrow arched door to the left of the fireplace. "Only the counselors and CITs know about this," she said. "But there's a secret passage in this closet." She pulled on a handle in the back wall, and a panel swung open to reveal a steep wooden staircase. The walls around the steps were brick, but the mortar looked gray and crumbly. "We suspect the device is hidden here."

Everyone surged forward.

"Wait," I said. "We need to do this in a logical way. Eugene and Ellen, you should go over the stairway, since you can find buried things. Maybe it will work with walls and stairs."

Ellen smiled—a nice smile. "Thanks, Stella," she whispered as she slipped past me.

"What about everyone else?" Ivan asked. He'd insisted on coming.

The others looked at me. It was a strange feeling. "Perhaps Garrett should touch the doorknobs and see if he can get any clues. The rest of us will search the old-fashioned way."

"Karen and I can lift heavy furniture," Jayden added. "Find us if you need us."

The other campers fanned out around the house, but I stood in the dining room, trying to figure out a plan. The entire camp was kidnapped—and by someone who was probably insane. I shivered.

Lindsey lingered behind with me. "He's not insane," she said softly. "But he'll do anything to get what he wants."

"Stella," called Jayden. "We've got something to show you."

I followed Jayden's voice up the stairs until I reached the attic. The walls were bare boards with plaster stuck between them. He stood in the middle of a dozen trunks and boxes where a window let in a wavery sunlight.

"It was Karen's idea," he said. "We told the boxes to move if they contained anything related to the Pandora Device, and this one jumped."

Karen pulled out a dress and held it up to her shoulders. "Looks old, doesn't it? I found something in the pocket." She handed me a letter dated 1692. "Look at the signature."

At the bottom in curly script was *Hepzibah*. I tried to read the rest, but the handwriting was too fancy.

"There's something more in the box," she said. She passed me a pocket-size notebook, the kind they sold in the camp store.

"This isn't as old as the dress," I said.

"And see the name on the first page—Dan Harski."

My mind tingled with possibilities. Perhaps we'd found a diary, and I could really know my dad at last. I turned to the next page, but it was just row after row of numbers with names of places beside them.

Jayden looked over my shoulder. "It's coming together," he said, his voice rising. "The scrap of paper from the dig site, Aunt Winnie's warning about your parents, and now this notebook—it adds up to some strange stuff."

"We need to figure out the letter," I said. "I wonder if Freddy could read it."

"I'll get him," he offered.

After he left, I flipped through the notebook, just more numbers and places—Salem, Alexandria, Frankfurt. I held it out to Karen. "Can you make anything of it?"

We were still puzzling over the pages when the boys sprinted up the stairs. "What can I read for you?" Freddy asked.

I handed him the letter, and he scrunched his face as he studied it. "Pretty thick cursive." His eyebrows rose in surprise. "It's addressed to Franny." He read slowly:

Dear Mistress Franny,

I endeavor to keep my Gift secret, but Neighbor Brown spied the candlelight when you visited last. She is asking questions, and I fear I will be accused a Witch. I will bury the gift you gave me. If this Misfortune comes to your knowledge, I trust you will do all you can to help me.

Your Friend,
Hepzibah

My breath caught at the closing line—*your friend*. "If Franny visited Hepzibah—"

Jayden whistled. "That would be time travel."

"And that's why Dr. Card wants the Pandora Device," I said. "We're looking for a time machine."

Karen folded the dress, her face puckered. "I can't tell you much, but Mr. Parker was concerned about something like this. He asked me to keep an eye on Stella in case anything happened." She put the dress in the trunk and closed it carefully. "We better keep this to ourselves until we know more."

I looked at the others, and they nodded in agreement.

Lindsey's voice called in my mind. *Stella, they need you in the kitchen.*

We hurried down the steps, and I thought how strange this day was becoming. I might not have a gift, but I was helping solve a huge problem. I was also beginning to understand why Aunt Winnie warned me to stop asking about my parents. My questions had put our whole camp in danger.

Eugene and Ellen joined us on the way to the kitchen, their hands covered in brick dust and a thundercloud forming on Eugene's brow. "We didn't find it," he said. "But we found lots of stupid notes that CITs from the past left behind loose bricks."

"Yeah—*Failure is simply the opportunity to begin again*," Ellen said in a mocking voice.

"It's probably a tradition," Eugene said. "Now, I'll have to come up with something intelligent to put there."

We arrived in the kitchen where Cecily and Coop were hunched over a gray mouse, which startled at our appearance and scampered through a hole in the corner.

"We might have a clue," she said, laughing. "It's the mice—silliest creatures that ever lived—Coop got them talking."

He ducked and blushed, but managed to speak up. "They said there's something big hidden in the wall."

"Which wall?"

"They didn't say, but their family territory is downstairs."

I stared at the bare kitchen walls and my vision blurred. I blinked, and a framed portrait seemed to appear on the white surface—the old colonel. "Remember the story of the curse and the hidden papers?" I asked.

I ran to the parlor, with everyone following, and tried to push an upholstered chair to the fireplace. Jayden took over, and it zipped into place without his even touching it.

"We need to look behind the portrait." I climbed the chair to stand on its broad back and stretched out my arms to either side of the frame.

"Wait," Karen said. "Let me check if it's booby-trapped, first." She reached with her palm toward the painting, drawing her hand back and forth. "It's attached to the wall, and there's a trip wire. Oops." A puff of smoke billowed around the frame. "Open it *now*."

I grabbed the portrait and pulled. The right side came forward, and I almost fell off the chair. More smoke leaked out, but I reached into the cavity behind the painting and found a thick package.

"It's going to explode," Karen cried.

We stumbled from the room as sparks shot from the frame, Eugene bellowing for everyone to get out of the house. We barely reached the front yard before an explosion burst behind us.

"What's going on?" Eugene demanded. Flames licked at the windows of the parlor.

"The frame was rigged," I said. I looked around and realized someone was missing. "Where's Ivan?"

He turned pale. "He was checking the furnace room."

146

Black smoke was pouring out of the house now.

"I'll get him," Jayden said.

Just then Ivan's lanky figure crossed the parlor window, his arms raised. If he stayed there any longer, he'd suffocate in the smoke.

"Jayden, can you open the window?"

He motioned with his hands, and the window snapped upward. Smoke spilled out, but strangely, the flames died down.

Ivan stuck his head through the window, a huge grin spread across his face. "Hey everyone—I'm going to be a fireman!" The smoke streaming around his shoulders made him cough, but he kept punching his fist in the air and laughing.

"Pull him out," Ellen said. "He's delirious."

We helped him climb out while Ivan talked the whole time. "You should've seen it, man. I just raised my arms, and the flames died out." His teeth shone white in his grimy face. "I found the use for my powers. Look inside."

We waited until the smoke cleared and then peered through the window. It was incredible. Except for the burned smell, you would never know a fire raged there. The portrait had swung closed, and only a few smudges on the frame gave any clue it was the source of the explosion.

I still held the bundle from behind the portrait, and now I lifted it for everyone to see. "We may have found what we're looking for."

I handed the cloth-wrapped package to Garrett, who rubbed his fingers across the surface. "Franny was here, and a guy named Dan. Bad things were happening. Men in white coats were chasing them." He stopped. "That's all there is. Should I open it?"

I nodded.

He pulled out something white. Lindsey and I looked at each other. Now I remembered where I'd seen the triangle-square logo. The machine was a clunky laptop, identical to the White Whale at home, except the logo in the corner wasn't scratched. I sent words to Lindsey's mind: *Don't tell anyone yet.* She placed a finger to her lips.

Jayden studied the gold lock that sealed the device. "Do you want me to open it?"

"No, we need more information," I said. "Garrett, can you tell us anything?"

Garrett's face twisted with confusion. "This is a time machine, and it brought Hepzibah here."

The others fell silent, staring at the laptop. Jayden stretched out a cautious hand to touch it. "A time machine," he said. "They're actually real."

"We can't let Dr. Card get hold of this," I said. "I'm not sure how to stop him, but there might be a clue in Buckeye's room."

"Let's go," said Ivan, lighting all ten fingers on fire.

∽✞∾

Back at Twain House, we split up to search Buckeye's room with Garrett standing by to take a reading on anything interesting.

"Do you mind if I study the notebook?" Karen asked. "It might be a code." I passed it to her, and she sat in the corner with a piece of paper, puzzling over the numbers.

"I've got something," Lindsey said, holding up a framed picture of two boys. The taller boy looked like a young version of Buckeye. He wore a safari hat and had his arm around the smaller boy.

Garrett felt the frame. "This is a happy memory," he said. "Buckeye with his little brother Bruce. They were going to be archeologists when they grew up . . . but it never happened. Bruce got sick. A rare cancer. He died a year later."

The ache for my parents came rushing back. I understood now why Buckeye said he had regrets.

"We have the information we need," I said. "Let's get something to eat." I didn't add that it might be our last meal for a long time.

"What a relief," Ellen said. "Buckeye's identical shirts were getting me down."

On the way to the dining hall Karen fell into step with me. "I have an idea about those numbers in the notebook. They might be dates and times, but they're written strangely."

I was only half-listening. I was developing an idea of my own. "Karen, do you think we could use the Pandora

Device to travel back in time and prevent the kidnapping today?"

"No!" I was surprised by the intensity in her voice. "If you don't believe anything else I say, believe this—you have to go forward to fix things. Overlapping time sets up a time loop that breaks history and triggers huge problems. That's why Mr. Parker was concerned about the unusual artifacts at our dig site. There are rules to this kind of thing."

I wondered if Buckeye saw it that way. For me, the idea of going back to save my parents made such rules useless.

"Read this." Karen pulled a folded sheaf of papers from her pocket. They were stapled together and worn at the edges as if she had carried them around for a while. "I tore them out of a book. It's a story by a guy named Ray Bradbury that shows what could happen if you change even something small in the past."

I studied the title: "A Sound of Thunder."

"I read this at school," I said. "A man traveled to prehistoric times and stepped on a butterfly, but when he got home everything was wrong."

She nodded. "Read it again."

I read the first few paragraphs, and it was strange how different the story seemed now. I decided to study it later. I stuffed the papers in my pocket and followed the others into the dining hall.

The cook was on the field trip, so we made sandwiches from cold cuts that Cecily found. Karen sat off to the side, still working on the notebook and barely touching the cheese and bread on her plate.

We were halfway through our sandwiches when a humming sound came through the windows. Coop looked out. "It's the buses—they're coming back!"

CHAPTER TWENTY-ONE

The campers waved and called to us as we ran to meet them. Kids poured from the buses, and Buckeye strode through the crowd, heading straight for me. "You have it?" His voice was low and urgent, and his eyes were too bright.

"It's b-back in the dining hall," I stammered.

"Take me there."

I sent out a silent call to Lindsey—we'd gotten separated—and I jogged to keep up with Buckeye.

"You can't trust those people, Buckeye. Who would kidnap busloads of kids for humanitarian reasons?"

He pushed the door with such force that it cracked against the doorstop. "They never knew they were kidnapped."

"But you don't believe all the stuff Dr. Card says, do you?"

"I joined for my own reasons."

He scanned the room, spotting the bundle on the table. Snatching it up, he tore off the cloth bag and warily studied the gold lock. "How do you open it?"

The door blew open again. Lindsey, Ellen and Jayden charged into the room.

"I need this opened!"

Jayden stepped forward. I admired how calm he appeared. "Let me try."

Lindsey was telegraphing words to me. *Stall him. The others are looking for Mr. Parker.*

Jayden waved his hands over the lock in slow motion. "It's a three layer lock with a booby trap at the end. If I don't do it right, I could destroy it."

Buckeye took off his safari hat and wiped his forehead with his arm. "You're the only chance I've got. Do it."

Trying not to catch his attention, I picked up the cloth bag and slipped the pages from Karen inside. "You'll want this," I said.

Buckeye's gaze never left the laptop as he put the bag in one of the large pockets of his khaki shirt.

"I've got the first layer," Jayden said.

"Buckeye, there's a reason this thing is called the Pandora Device," I said.

He jumped. "How'd you know the name?"

"Remember the note you sent us? We met your boss."

"He's not my boss anymore."

"That's why you need to read the papers I put in the bag."

"Stella, it's nice of you to try. But there's something I have to do."

"Second level," Jayden said.

"Faster," urged Buckeye.

"We saw the picture of your brother," I said. "You can't save his life if he has cancer. Even if you go back in time."

"Third level—I think I've disarmed the booby trap." Jayden took a breath and cautiously raised the lid. The laptop blinked to life.

With a cry, Buckeye grabbed the machine. His fingers flew over the keys, and then he paused and looked up. The sadness on his face made me gasp. He pushed a button. Light flashed in the place he had stood, and thunder roared.

My ears were still ringing when the door crashed open and three large men strode in. They wore jeans and T-shirts as though they belonged to the camp, but I saw the brown square-toed shoes on their feet.

"Stella Harski? You're coming with us."

"Where are you taking her?" Jayden demanded. Out of the corner of my eye I saw the bug juice cooler levitating toward the man's head.

"She's wanted at the laboratory."

The other two men edged around the room, surrounding us.

"Run," Jayden shouted, as the cooler knocked into the first man.

We dashed for the kitchen, and I heard the crack and slosh of the juice cooler as it slammed into the second man, and then the third. But when we pushed open the back door, our cook stood there. He zapped us with a small silver box, and my limbs went stiff. Jayden tried to summon the dish pans, but the pulse from the contraption surged again, and everything went black.

❧

I woke up in a white room with seemingly no corners or door. Lindsey, Ellen and Jayden lay a few feet away. Lindsey's eyes opened.

"You okay?" I asked.

She touched a lump on her forehead. "I must have fallen." She surveyed the room with a dazed expression.

Ellen stirred, but Jayden lay frighteningly still. I reached for his wrist to check his pulse, but he sat up, clutching his stomach. "Something's wrong," he said.

I realized my stomach was cramping as well. "That thing that zapped us," I said.

Ellen pushed herself up and rubbed her arm. "I'm going to have huge bruises tomorrow."

Something whirred above us, and a panel slid open to send a computer screen down from the ceiling.

The head of Dr. Card appeared on it. "Welcome, again, Miss Harski," he said. "I thought you would have brought me the machine by now, but alas, events have conspired against us."

"Buckeye took it," I said. "Wasn't he bringing it to you?"

"Tut, tut. I hate lying."

The floor glowed, and a current of electricity coursed through my body. Lindsey groaned and went limp. Jayden jumped up and levitated our bodies from the ground.

"Nicely done, but you need to follow instructions better if you are going to work for me."

My arms ached from the blast. "We're not working for you," I shouted.

The screen went blank, and the glow from the floor dimmed as the monitor receded back into the ceiling. Jayden grunted and lowered us to the ground, just as Lindsey woke up again. I tried to help her sit.

"I'm okay," she said. "I was trying to reach his thoughts, but he slammed me back, and I blacked out."

"What do we do next?" asked Ellen.

"I don't know, but they may be listening." I looked at Lindsey and sent a message to her: *Can you tell the others to communicate through your mind?*

Lindsey got Jayden and Ellen to look at her, and they nodded in understanding. We sat cross-legged on the floor in a tight square. My mind chugged furiously. The white walls probably meant we were back at the lab. *Ellen, can you see what's behind the ceiling?*

She closed her eyes, tilting her head back. *There's a guard in the room up there, watching a monitor on a desk.*

That gave me an idea. *Ask Jayden if he can knock out the guard. We might escape through the trap door.*

Jayden crouched as though ready to spring and then levitated to the ceiling, pushing back the panel in one smooth motion. His head and shoulders disappeared through the gap, and a terrific crash sounded above us.

"Come on up—" He levitated the three of us through the opening, and we landed in a heap next to him.

In the corner the guard lay unconscious with a broken monitor by his head.

Lindsey blinked and spoke aloud. "It's safe to talk now, but someone just contacted us. Her name is Sarah, and she's a prisoner like us. She wants us to go to her."

I wondered if Dr. Card would trap us with a story like this. No, his traps would be more spectacular. I cracked the door an inch and looked into the hallway. The same glaring white walls stretched in both directions. "Ask how we can find her," I said.

Lindsey slipped into the passage and drifted to the left. "She says to walk till we reach a door with a small window near the ground."

"This place is getting creepier all the time," Ellen said.

I tiptoed behind Lindsey, wishing I could shrink to mouse-size. If someone spotted us, there would be nowhere to hide.

"We're getting closer," Lindsey murmured.

"It's like that game, 'hot and cold'," Jayden whispered. "Wait." He crouched down and slipped aside the panel to a small window. "We found her."

I tried the doorknob, but it was locked. "Can you open it?"

It took Jayden so long I began to imagine guards chasing us down the long white hall, but finally the lock clicked, and a tall woman with ebony skin greeted us. She wore an orange headscarf and a flowing gown that swirled with orange, blue and purple.

"Come in quick," she said.

The light in her room was dimmer, and every inch of the wall was covered with paintings that matched the bright design of her robe. She saw my admiring glance. "All that white was driving me crazy."

"Did they bring you here to make these?" I asked.

She snorted. "No, they brought me here to create things—silly stuff like machines—I'd rather be painting." She hurriedly passed out white lab coats. "You'll need these for our escape. It's time to get the others."

"Who are the others?" I asked.

"Other prisoners, brought here to work for the Human Project." She was talking faster now. "Harold predicts the future and said we had to wait for you."

She hustled us through the door and down the passage, but Ellen froze by one of the doors. "There's someone here."

Sarah frowned. "There shouldn't be, unless they brought a new prisoner today."

I touched the door, and my vision wobbled. "We need to find out who's inside," I said.

Jayden unlocked the door faster this time, and in the dim room we found an old woman lying on a bed.

Aunt Winnie.

❧❧

CHAPTER TWENTY-TWO

❧❧

With great effort, Aunt Winnie pushed herself into a sitting position. "Stella, how did you find me?" Her forehead wrinkled as her eyes tried to focus.

"They brought us here, too, and we're escaping."

She shook her head. "I'm too weak, and my wheelchair is gone."

I held her hand. "We can get you out." I looked at Jayden, and he nodded.

He scooped up Aunt Winnie, and we rushed from the room.

"Thank you," she murmured. It seemed to take all her strength just to speak. Her body went limp in Jayden's arms.

Sarah prodded us to walk faster to the next cell. When Jayden unlocked it, a man peered around the door. He had two tufts of hair above his ears, and his bald head glowed in the light from the room beyond. "This is Harold," she said.

Harold gave a little jump and slid into the hallway. "Time at last!" He wore striped pajamas and carried a

bundle of clothes. "As you can see, I'm always prepared."
I liked him at once.

Suddenly he clapped a hand to his forehead. "Come inside quickly." He closed the door behind us, and a minute later the tapping of footsteps sounded a few feet away.

Sarah shook her finger at him. "Good thing you knew the guards were coming. Now, you better put on a lab coat over those pajamas."

He sniffed. "I don't see you wearing one."

"That's because I always dress like this." She held his bundle while he put on the lab coat. His striped pajamas stuck out from the bottom, and I didn't think he would be very convincing if we met the guards. But then, Jayden carrying Aunt Winnie would be suspicious, too.

"Do the others know?" Sarah asked.

"They will when we get to the lab," he replied, his eyes twinkling.

"You predicted this was going to happen—you're supposed to alert everyone."

His face fell. "I'm not good at the mental transference stuff, but then I thought—it will be more of a surprise this way."

"Lindsey can do it," I said.

Harold mumbled how people didn't appreciate surprises anymore, but Sarah folded her arms. "Thank you, Lindsey. You'll want to contact Cliff."

Lindsey closed her eyes. "Got him."

"Tell him to get the others and meet us in the tunnel."

The tunnel lay behind a gray door—rough cinderblock walls and dim bulbs. The bright colors of Sarah's gown swept ahead of us, and we walked faster to keep up. I held Aunt Winnie's hand while Jayden floated her at his side, like she was riding an invisible stretcher. "I wish we could do something to help her," I said.

"We are doing something," Jayden said. "We're getting her out of here."

The dim bulbs blinked twice, and Sarah gasped. "They've discovered our escape. We need to find the passage to the lab—fast!" She strode ahead and began frantically running her hands over the wall. "It should be here somewhere."

"I can find it," Ellen said. She walked along the passage, hands outstretched. "It's here." There was no door frame or any hint of an opening, but Jayden rubbed the patch of wall, and a tall chunk of cinderblock swung inward.

Sarah ducked through the door. "Close it after us—it will keep us safe a little longer."

I ran to catch up with her, but Harold caught my arm. "Bad turn—no—guards ahead," he mumbled. He rubbed his bald head. "Too many possibilities."

"Maybe you should just focus on our group," I said. "Where are we going now?"

He looked up in surprise, then peered down the tunnel. "Why—forward, of course."

"And who will we meet at the end?"

He started mumbling again. "Three people...or... no one...or the doctor...or...."

A lantern flashed ahead.

"Ahoy there," a voice called out. "What's been keeping you?"

Harold perked up. "Definitely three people."

A giant of a man emerged from the shadows, holding the lantern high, and two more people in white lab coats followed. One lab coat featured the monogram of an "M" and the other a "C." They were barely older than us, and they were identical twins.

"I had to twist their arms to make them leave," the large man said. "Melvin was close to a breakthrough, and Calvin was programming it on the computer."

"How many times do I have to tell you, we don't want a breakthrough," Sarah said.

Melvin scratched his forehead. "When we're working, we forget everything else."

His brother shrugged. "We can't stop ourselves."

"It's time to escape," she continued briskly. "Cliff, these are the young people we were waiting for."

Cliff strode forward and shook our hands. "Freedom at last."

"How are you planning to escape?" I asked.

Sarah's eyebrows rose almost to the orange scarf she wore in her hair. "Harold said your team would know."

"Us?" I asked.

Harold began sputtering. "It *is* a possibility."

162

I peered through the dimness—thick cinderblock walls, miles of passageways and hidden doors we knew nothing about. What were they thinking?

The lights flashed again, three flashes this time, and I shivered. If we were going to escape in time, we needed to collect everything we knew. I remembered Lindsey's story about her class. "Lindsey, can you help us share information?"

Sarah stepped toward her. "Share my information first."

Lindsey closed her eyes, and the next moment, images began flowing through my brain. They came rapidly, like snatches of a movie in fast-forward: Dr. Card and his men, people wearing lab coats, and dozens of blinking machines.

"Me next," said Harold.

The movie slowed for a moment. These pictures seemed murkier. Several times the sequence of events started over and ended differently.

"Wait," I said. "I see a pair of shoes."

"They wouldn't do you any good," interjected Melvin. "They have to be programmed to go somewhere."

"Could you do that?" I asked.

He stared at me wonderingly. "Well, I suppose it's possible."

"Once we start working on something…" Calvin said.

"We can't help figuring things out," Melvin finished.

Cliff set the lantern on the ground. "The prototype pair is with the other inventions in cabinets, but they're locked. We wouldn't have time to search them all."

"We can do it," I said. "Ellen can find things, and Jayden will take care of the lock." I looked at the twins. "Could one pair of shoes transport all of us?"

"Oh yes," Melvin said. "If we're going to the same place."

Sarah stared at me with a peculiar expression. "Harold was right about you."

I felt myself blushing and hoped she didn't notice in the dim light.

"We have to hurry," Cliff said. "I'll take these two. If we don't make it back, continue without us."

☙☙

CHAPTER TWENTY-THREE

☙☙

Melvin pulled out a small apparatus and began typing on it. "We'll program the code for our escape," he explained.

I held Aunt Winnie's hand and softly called her name. Slowly, she opened her eyes. "Are you okay?"

Her face wrinkled in a smile. "I'm fine, child. They drugged me when they brought me here, but I'm feeling better."

The lights were signaling more urgently now—four flashes after each interval. With every set of flashes I worried the lights would cut off permanently. I got the rest of the group to sit in a circle so we'd be ready when the others returned.

Lindsey sat next to Harold, who rocked back and forth, his head bowed in his hands. "I just don't know," he said.

"Don't think about it," she said. "Cast your mind the other way and concentrate on something happy in your past."

He raised his head. "There was my mother's chocolate cake, and mashed potatoes and gravy."

"That's the idea." Lindsey gave him an encouraging nod.

He closed his eyes, and his face grew calm, but Lindsey jumped to her feet. "Ellen says to get ready."

We stood and held hands with Sarah supporting Aunt Winnie, whose eyes sparkled with determination. She winked at me, and I felt an extra surge of courage.

Jayden appeared first, running toward us with the shoes tucked under his arm. I'd forgotten how fast he could run.

"Melvin, are you done programming?" I asked.

His fingers flew over the keyboard. "Almost."

Jayden handed the shoes to him and joined the ring.

Cliff and Ellen arrived, and eager hands grasped theirs to complete the circle while from the far end of the tunnel a light exploded.

"Now!" Cliff bellowed.

"Program uploaded," Melvin said. "Everyone concentrate on our destination."

Lindsey sent the image. She held Harold's hand, and he was muttering again, but when he got her picture, he stopped and grinned. "It just might work."

Melvin jammed on the shoes, and I grabbed his hand. The familiar buzzing sent a tingling like electricity through our circle. The cinder block walls turned transparent, and the hazy outlines of Ivan's bed began to form.

But something was wrong. We were moving too slowly. A concrete wall rose in front of us, and we slammed into it as a white light pulsed and wind whipped us backwards.

Harold kept repeating "Oh no," until with a jolt we stopped, and the shoes sparked on Melvin's feet. We were standing, still holding hands, in the laboratory with Dr. Card and his men surrounding us.

"Trying to escape?" Dr. Card said.

"Unbroken," muttered Harold "Let the circle be unbroken—unbroken still the ties..." I took a tighter grip of Melvin on my other side.

"Ah, the beauty of the override function," Dr. Card said. "And what is this? You repay my hospitality, Stella, by taking my best workers?"

"I'm not taking them. You're breaking the law—holding people against their will."

"Against their will? I thought my people were happiest here." He flicked his wrist, and two of his men pulled me from the circle and shoved me toward him. "And you are going to be the happiest of them all."

He stared at me, and I wondered how long I could hold out with the pressure of his thoughts trying to invade my brain.

"You are a nuisance, Stella Harski, but fortunately for you, my laboratory has almost perfected reading the future." His voice was quiet, but his eyes reminded me of Buckeye when he stole the Pandora Device. "We have a 98% certainty that you will bring the machine here." His white teeth flashed again.

"You can't control me," I said, trying to sound confident.

"Actually, I can. What do you want more than anything else in the world? Perhaps you want to be a scientist—push back the borders of knowledge?"

Lindsey's words floated into my mind. *It's not what he thinks.* I blinked, and the force of his probing grew weaker.

Dr. Card brought out a thick binder. "We've been watching you for years. You live in a house that should have been condemned, with your elderly grandmother, who is not quite fit to take care of you, is she?"

That old heavy feeling in my chest returned, but I resisted the urge to take a deep breath. I stared at the ground and mustered every image I could of Grandma. Her face beaming with delight when she brought home a treat for me... her soothing voice reading from the newspaper. Grandma, sitting in her recliner, eating from a TV tray while I told her about school.

Dr. Card's voice glided on, but I barely listened until I caught the word *parents*. "We could do that, you know— send you back in time to be with them, when they were first married and happy. Before the accident took them away."

I glanced at Lindsey, and she frowned. Everyone was still holding hands, but the circle seemed to wobble. Her voice shot into my head.

Trust yourself.

My double vision cleared, and the truth exploded in my brain. "It wasn't an accident that killed them, was it?" I said. "Your organization did it. You did it to get something." And I knew what it was—the Pandora Device.

I wanted to yell, but I forced my voice to stay calm. "Problems aren't solved by going backward. Even if you sent me back, we wouldn't have long to live." Dr. Card's gaze felt like it was boring a hole in my head, making me feverish. I had to do something before I lost the ability to think. "If your experts know I will bring you the device, let everyone else go," I said.

Dr. Card raised an eyebrow, as if I was holding him up for all his money. "What? Let my best workers go? And who knows what your little friends might accomplish for me?"

A swift thought shot from Lindsey. *What are you doing?*

I gritted my teeth and continued. "We can do quite a lot, and you won't get what you want if you keep the rest of them here. Do you really want that machine?"

Dr. Card studied our group. Harold was muttering, Melvin and Calvin were looking vacantly into space, and Ellen glared back at him.

He turned to the man beside him. "What do you say, Henri? Are the probabilities higher with or without the friends?"

Henri stared at my face for an entire minute. I raised my chin in the air and tried to look like Ellen when she was determined.

"Without friends," he said at last.

"Very well. I know where to find them, after all." Dr. Card brushed his hand toward our circle. "Be gone."

The shoes on Melvin's feet glowed, and sparks ran up his legs and out his arms until the entire circle appeared to be on fire.

Jayden says we'll bring help—Lindsey sent the message so powerfully that blue spots danced in front of my eyes. The circle shimmered in space for a moment and then disappeared.

I exhaled slowly.

"Now," Dr. Card said. "We wait for the device."

His men closed in around me. I stared at the floor, trying to keep Dr. Card from prying into my mind. I concentrated on Lindsey's message—*Trust yourself.* Somehow I'd known what to say to Dr. Card to convince him to let the others go. Was that what she meant?

My thoughts were like a wall against Dr. Card, and around me the lab grew quiet. Only the whirrings and clickings of machines told me I was still there. I glanced up warily.

Dr. Card was watching me as if I was an insect under glass. A sly smile curled his lips. "Have you ever wondered why your grandmother was so different?" he asked. "Stockpiling newspapers and socks and pans?"

I pressed my lips together. I didn't trust myself to speak.

"She has all the symptoms of being caught in a time loop, but until your invitation to camp, we couldn't discover why. That's why you're so important, Stella. You're going to bring me the device."

I tried to steady my voice. "A 98% chance sounds pretty certain to me. I should have it any time now." The relief over sending my friends to safety was making me giddy. "Of course, it's an interesting fact about probabilities. You can have a 90% chance of sunshine, and it rains anyway."

Dr. Card glowered, and I forced a giggle. I was trying to come up with more to say when the key chain around my neck seemed to spark. I pulled it out and felt it burning in my palm. The next moment, the room shook and lights flashed. Gusts of wind blew hundreds of papers through the air, and the men rushed to protect Dr. Card.

I leaned against the wind and edged away from them until my back pressed against one of the lab tables. With a final blast of thunder, a cluster of people appeared beside me. The wind stopped, and the papers fluttered to the ground. In the stillness I saw our team: Jayden, Lindsey and Ellen, and with them—a girl and a boy. They were older, about the age of Cecily and Eugene.

The boy was holding the Pandora Device.

He turned, and I recognized him. It was my father. And the girl was my mother. My knees sagged, and I gripped the table.

My mother was a little taller than me and had the same fringe of brown hair, but where my chin was square, hers was pointed. Her wide-spaced eyes met mine. I'd always thought I must be a lot like her, but in that glance I saw the face of a dreamer, not the practical scientist I'd always imagined.

My father was one of those gangly guys, whose arms seem too long. He grinned at Dr. Card, the corners of his mouth curving upward as though he thought this was a joke. "How nice to see you again, Dr. Card."

Dr. Card moved toward the machine, but my father put up a hand. "Not so fast. We need to know you'll let us go unharmed."

Dr. Card took another step. "If you don't give me the device..."

"What? From where I'm standing we're pretty untouchable." The boy tapped his forehead. "I can see the possibilities, you know."

A faint smile passed across my mother's lips, and she reached out and took my hand. "I'm Franny, and this is Dan," she murmured.

When she touched me, a jolt of excitement flowed through my skin. I wanted to hug her and tell her who I was, but Ellen grabbed me from the other side. "Not now," she said, her voice urgent. "I'll explain later."

Franny stretched out her arms and two tables slid into place, separating us from Dr. Card. At the same time, Jayden raised his hands, and the shiny instruments on the tables launched themselves at Dr. Card and his men. They yelled and tried to fend off the attack of screwdrivers and wrenches, which swarmed around their heads like hornets. The thug, who had been our cook, swiped his arms through the air, and the tools fell to the ground in a pinging clatter.

"GIVE me the device…it belongs to me," Dr. Card demanded, his voice so low it practically vibrated. The words repeated over and over, and I realized I was hearing them in my head. My hands twitched toward the device, and Dan edged forward, but Lindsey stepped in front of us. The droning stopped as quickly as if headphones had been ripped from my ears.

Ellen pulled us back toward the group, talking quietly as she did. "There's a tunnel under this room, and they're sending men to surround us. We need to leave now."

"Got it," said Dan. "I'm almost ready." He typed frantically into the device.

"No!" yelled Dr. Card. He snatched up a screwdriver and leapt across the table, swinging it at Dan. The screwdriver punctured his arm. I screamed, and Jayden launched himself at Dr. Card, pinning him to the ground. His men started forward, but he growled at them to stay back. "Don't wreck the possibilities."

Blood trickled from Dan's wound, and I pulled out the screwdriver and clamped his arm with my hand. As I touched him, my brain exploded. It was like a slide show gone crazy with images popping up one after another faster than I could fully take them in: our team running with the device, Dr. Card's face washed with a greenish light, me with my parents alive—eating dinner together, going to the beach, riding in a car. Then, a horrific crash, a car beneath a giant truck, another picture of Dr. Card holding the Pandora Device, a crowd of people cheering and waving flags.

Dan looked at me, astonished. "You've got the gift," he said. "Sort the possibilities before they get away." He gripped his good hand over mine. "Start with Dr. Card—what does he want?"

I was still in shock over what was happening, but I concentrated on the last image of Dr. Card. "He wants the device. No, there's more—he wants power."

The slide show reversed in slow motion, and the picture of Dr. Card clutching the device returned.

"Hold that one," said Dan. "And work backwards."

It took all my strength, but I felt the energy from Dan, pushing the slides back, one by one. At last we reached a slide I hadn't seen before—a picture of me with the device.

Dan was sweating and his face turned a pasty white. "Branch forward," he whispered. I didn't know what he meant, but his fingers curled more tightly around mine, and slowly the picture split in two. In the one on the left, I gave the device to Dr. Card, and in the other I gave it to Dan. The two branches began to advance through a series of images, slow at first and then faster and faster, and only one branch led to stopping Dr. Card.

Dan was breathing heavily now. He nodded his head. "Do it." He pushed a few keys on the device and handed it to me.

I stepped forward and placed it on the floor by Dr. Card.

For a moment time seemed to stand still. Then Dr. Card, his face wild, wrenched his arm free from Jayden and pressed a button on the machine. A light flashed and thunder cracked.

Jayden sprang away from him, and Ellen grabbed his hand. "I've got the shoes—everyone together!"

We caught hands, completing the circle, just as a trap door flew open, and Dr. Card's thugs poured out.

"Go to Jayden's house," I shouted. Flames spurted from the shoes, running in a fiery path around our circle. Then a roaring filled my ears, and the lab zipped away into blackness. The rumbling grew until we landed with a final shock in Jayden's yard, where the first pink streaks of dawn stretched across the sky.

CHAPTER TWENTY-FOUR

"We did it!" Jayden yelled, and Lindsey and Ellen hugged me.

"I hope you have a good explanation for what you did," Ellen said.

I didn't answer. I was mesmerized with Franny and Dan. He collapsed onto the grass, and she whipped off her bandana to wrap around his arm. He laughed and told her not to worry. I watched them, trying to soak in every movement, every word.

Ellen pulled me aside, speaking fast and low. "Karen sent a message for you—you can't tell your parents who you are. Too much knowledge is risky in time travel."

The airy excitement that filled my lungs leaked away, replaced with a heaviness in the pit of my stomach. I wanted to shout "Mom and Dad—it's me Stella!" but instead my voice choked, and I barely whispered, "Thanks for saving me."

"Glad to," Franny said. "A couple of my trackers lit up, and we came to help."

"Trackers?"

"The key chain you're wearing."

Ellen brought out her key chain, and I felt for the cord at my neck. The tracker was still warm.

"Karen figured out the code in Dan's notebook," Ellen said. "The dig site was the time portal, and Dan recorded an entry for today."

"Did Mr. Parker know?" I asked.

"No. He was busy sorting out Sarah and the others. But Jayden started running, and we followed. We never would've made contact if Lindsey hadn't reached out to Dan's mind."

"An impressive bit of thought transference," he said. "We found each other, and with your tracker, it was easy to find you."

"But why in the world did you give the Pandora Device to Dr. Card?" Ellen demanded.

I looked at Dan, and the warmth of his smile gave me confidence. "I found my gift—I can see possibilities, and I saw the way to stop him."

The color was coming back to Dan's face. "I programmed the machine so it will only go forward a day at a time." He chuckled. "It will take Dr. Card a while to figure out how to override it, and in the meantime, we know where the present-day version of the Pandora Device is hidden. We're going to retrieve it so we can take it back to our own time and destroy it. Permanently. Dr. Card will find himself without a time machine."

"Are you sure it will work?" Ellen asked.

"Yes—it's the nature of Stella's gift to see the possibilities."

"Which brought us here?" she asked. She shot me a warning look, reminding me not to give away my identity.

"It's the easiest way to get the device," I said. "It's in Franny's old house. Follow me."

We crept up the stairs as quietly as we could, but when we reached the landing Grandma called from her bedroom. "Who's there?"

I whispered to the others to wait for me, and I walked into her room.

"Stella," she cried, clasping my hands.

She looked weak, and a sudden fear clutched my heart. "Are you all right?"

"Of course," she said. "But I've had the strangest dreams. You were coming for the White Whale because the Englishman said it wasn't safe."

"Who..." I began, but Grandma caught her breath. I followed her gaze and saw Franny standing in the doorway.

"Franny, is that you?" She dropped back against her pillows, closing her eyes. Her face turned deathly white. "I'm still dreaming," she murmured.

Franny stood frozen, but Dan pulled her away. "We need to work quickly," he said, motioning to me.

I squeezed Grandma's hand and followed.

We took the stairs two at a time, Franny muttering to Dan, who seemed to be arguing. I only caught the words "too dangerous."

The White Whale lay on my bookcase, and I scooped it up and gave it to Dan.

"Thanks," he said. He studied my face as though searching for something. "I suspect there are more connections here than we guessed." Then he held up a hand. "But don't tell us—we don't want to mess up the future."

Franny grabbed me by the shoulders and hugged me fiercely. "I wish we had more time," she said.

I clung to her for a moment.

"I'll see you again someday," she whispered.

I forced back a sob. For me, this was the last time. In my future, I would never see her again.

"You did the right thing, Stella." The gentleness in his voice soaked through my skin and down to my bones. He brushed my hand, and a dozen pictures flashed before my eyes. "All good possibilities," he said.

My mother let go of me and took his hand. He pushed a button on the White Whale. Thunder rumbled and lightning flashed.

They were gone.

The energy drained from my legs. I stumbled, and Lindsey caught me. "We need to get you back to camp," she said.

"I've got to check on Grandma first."

I didn't mean for her to see me, but she must have been watching the doorway. "Stella, this is for you. In my dream I'm supposed to give it to you."

It was a clipping from the newspaper with the headline "New Technology Saves Lives" and underneath a photo of young Buckeye with his arm around his little brother. Behind them stood a familiar figure.

I sank onto the bed, and Grandma held my hand while I read the caption: "Bruce Jaeger with his brother and Uncle 'Buckeye,' who donated the bone marrow that saved his life."

"He made it back," I murmured.

Grandma patted the paper. "It's the Englishman. Friend of your parents. He died in the crash with them."

I kissed her cheek. "You should rest."

"I know," she said, smiling. "I've been having the most wonderful dreams." She lay back and closed her eyes.

◈

Lindsey used thought transference to contact Mr. Parker, and he rode with the bus that came to pick us up. He burst through the door and shook our hands enthusiastically. "You four gave me quite a scare," he said. "But I'm glad you're safe."

We took turns telling him everything that happened. The worry lines in his forehead relaxed when he heard that Franny and Dan went back to destroy the machine. I gave him Grandma's newspaper clipping, too.

"Buckeye did the right thing in the end," he said. "He planted the Pandora Device where we would find it."

"What about the Human Project?" Jayden asked.

"Thanks to Melvin and Calvin, we traced the location, and our agents raided the lab. They seized the equipment, but Dr. Card and his people escaped."

In my mind, I saw Dr. Card again, stabbing my father, and I cringed.

Mr. Parker must have seen the panic on my face. "He can't do much without his lab, and the authorities are pursuing him now." He fixed us with his unblinking stare. "Which reminds me, they've asked us to keep the details of Dr. Card and the Human Project a secret. That means we won't be able to say anything about this at camp."

I thought of Ivan lighting his fingers on fire and cackling over our discovery of the time machine. "Does the rest of our group know?"

"They do. Even Ivan." I wondered if he'd read my mind.

The bus shot through Simmons Tunnel, but the craziness of the ride was lost on me. I felt as though I'd left part of myself behind. Buckeye and my parents were in the past now.

As we emerged from the tunnel, Ellen slipped into the seat beside me. "I thought you might want to have this," she said. It was the cloth case from the Pandora Device, more grimy than I remembered it. "I found it near the front door, and there's something inside for you."

I pulled out the stapled pages of Bradbury's short story. Written across the top in blue pen was a simple message. "Thank you, Stella."

Ellen smiled, and I realized we were now friends.

CHAPTER TWENTY-FIVE

The next morning Mr. Parker invited me to his office. Aunt Winnie was already there, sitting in her wheel chair.

"Aunt Winnie tells me you've found your gift," he said.

I blushed. "I used to worry my invitation here was a mistake, but after all that's happened, I realize I don't need a special gift to help."

"That lesson is a gift in itself."

I looked at him, and his image wobbled. I was embarrassed that I always seemed on the brink of passing out.

"That double-vision is part of your gift," he said.

I'd forgotten that Mr. Parker could read minds. "It doesn't feel like a gift."

"It's only a symptom. When your vision goes double, it's because two strands of reality are splitting in front of you. You're seeing the possibilities, like you did in Dr. Card's lab. I knew you had this gift the first time I met you—the way you saw possibilities in going to camp, and then possibilities in your friends when you wanted them to come."

I tried to take in his words, but it didn't make sense. "What good is a gift that makes you black-out all the time?"

"Your gift is immature," he said. "But if you train it, you'll see more and more clearly, and the black-outs will recede over time."

I turned to Aunt Winnie. "That's why you told me to close my eyes when I got dizzy and concentrate on what I was seeing…"

She nodded, her eyes glowing with hidden laughter. "And when you did, you probably knew what to do." She tapped my arm. "Meet me at my cabin tomorrow for your first craft class."

"You're my teacher?"

"I told you this gift was rare, didn't I? I haven't had a camper to teach since your father was here." She pulled an envelope from her pocket. "He gave me this shortly after you were born. He knew you'd come one day, and he wanted you to have this when you discovered your gift."

I held the envelope and studied the precise letters that spelled my name—the handwriting of a scientist. I would save it until I could be alone.

While the others attended classes, I walked down to the lake, empty now. I sat in one of the green canoes that lay on the shore and looked out at the sparkling waters ringed with pine trees and blue sky. I opened the envelope and read:

Dear Stella,

If you get this letter, it means that your mother and I are no longer with you. We are doing everything we can to stay safe for your sake, but there are some possibilities we cannot avoid.

We have loved you from the moment you were born, and we hope you will always remember this. As I write, you are learning to sit up and have even said a few syllables, which your mother assures me are "Daddy."

We're sorry this message could not be delivered to you earlier, but we could not risk the Pandora Device being found. We have written other letters that will be delivered at the right times. For now, we want you to know that we are very proud of you. Congratulations on finding your gift. As you develop your abilities, use them to seek what is true and right.

Love,
Daddy and Mom

కించి

CHAPTER TWENTY-SIX

కించి

The last week of camp was blissfully uneventful, unless you count the cream pie levitating contest—in which everyone came out so sticky we had to swim in the lake—or the pig calling competition—who knew pigs were so smart? My favorite was board game night. Every team had someone who could read hidden writing. Freddy was on our team, and we won twenty points for Hawthorne House, partly because Jayden was an incredible strategist.

Midweek we cleaned up Aunt Winnie's house as a service project. We swept up broken pots and brought her new jars full of wild flowers, and she sat in her wheelchair, directing the work. While I was putting books back on the shelves, I found an old album of photographs from the years my parents were at camp. Cecily sat with Aunt Winnie and me as we pored over the pictures.

"Look, it's my mother," she said. "Aunt Winnie, did you know someone named Sibby?"

"I did," she said, adjusting her glasses. "But in those days we called her Hepzibah."

Cecily's eyes widened. "She wasn't the one…"

"Yes, she was," Aunt Winnie said with a laugh. "And my, oh my, she was a character."

Cecily peered closer at the picture of the girl called Hepzibah. "I knew my mother was old-fashioned, but I didn't know she was *really* old-fashioned."

"Here's another one you've met," Aunt Winnie said. "He came with Hepzibah because his mother was hanged as a witch. Ethan Card."

My breath caught in my throat. I looked at Aunt Winnie, and she nodded slowly. I knew she meant for me to understand something, but my memories of Dr. Card were still too painful.

Sarah and the other practitioners from the lab stayed for the week to give seminars on their areas of expertise. Cliff could control fire, and Ivan learned so much from him that by the end of the week he could start the campfire while he was a hundred yards away, splashing in the lake. Sarah taught oil painting, and Melvin and Calvin revolutionized the robotics teams. But Harold's seminar was on fishing. "Fishing is always a surprise," he told me. "And that's worth all the effort."

Though Eugene took the dowsing class back to the dig site three more times, they didn't find any further artifacts, except for a tattered old bandana, stained brown. I thought of my parents' last trip, and I knew where it came from.

On the last night we celebrated with a huge bonfire. Mr. Parker awarded a silver trophy to the Fellows for winning the most points, and the Thornes came in second.

"Thornes!" yelled Ivan, lighting all ten fingers on fire.

"Thornes," we echoed.

"Just wait till next year," Eugene growled.

The thought of next summer made saying good-bye a little easier.

Back at the dorm I packed everything up. My picture frame was still empty from the prank the first night, but now I had a memory of my parents that was even better. I tucked the letter from my dad in the frame, and felt for my mother's key chain around my neck. It was nice to remember there was a tracking device inside that had led her to me.

I had made a dozen new key chains, and I put them in a brown bag so they would be ready the next day.

At breakfast I gave them to everyone at our table. Ellen blushed when I handed her one. "I'm sorry I don't have anything for you," she said.

"That's okay. It's just a memento."

"So it doesn't have a tracker like your mom's key chain?" Jayden asked.

"Memory is a kind of tracker," Lindsey said, twirling my gift from her finger as though it was one of her dream catchers.

Karen frowned. "I have something for you, too." She passed me a white envelope with my name in block letters.

"Those warning letters—they were from you?"

"I'm sorry—Mr. Parker asked me to keep you safe and prevent you from stirring up interest in your parents. I guess I overdid it."

I opened the envelope and pulled out the old photograph of Franny and Dan.

"The prank was you, too?"

I felt bad I'd suspected Joanne that first night, but then I looked in her direction. She was leading her group in a game to torment Ivan by levitating his suitcase out of his reach. Karen followed my gaze, and the suitcase flipped upside down, the handle thumping Joanne's head.

She screamed and scanned the room to find who did it, but Karen was already looking at her plate, her whole concentration focused on cutting her piece of sausage.

After breakfast everyone exchanged contact information so we could keep in touch. Ivan had only his address to give us. "We don't have electricity where I live," he said, "or phones."

"Will you come next year?" I asked.

His face broke into a grin. "Of course, and I'll bring the rest of my team."

Mr. Parker walked with me to the bus. "Stella, I want to thank you for what you did. I guess you understand now why we didn't want you to learn about your parents. There was too much at stake if Dr. Card got hold of the Pandora Device."

I nodded. "Like the story Hawthorne wrote. All the evils of the world set free."

He gave me one of his lopsided smiles. "Do you know the ending of that story about Pandora's Box? After all the evil came out, there was one more creature left in the box—Hope."

The door snapped shut, and the bus creaked down the driveway. I waved to Mr. Parker until we turned onto the dirt road and the trees closed in around us. We passed beneath the log arch, and the camp sign grew smaller and smaller as we drove toward the railway tunnel.

Lindsey's mother met the bus and offered to take everyone home. I should have been suspicious when she pulled onto our street and dozens of people filled our yard. Miss Charlotte was passing out glasses of lemonade, and Lindsey's father was standing over a grill. Ellen's parents and some neighbors clustered around a collection of Grandma's old tables, arranging plates of cupcakes, carrot sticks and potato chips.

As we got out of the car, everyone clapped and shouted "Welcome home," and Grandma stretched out her arms for a hug. "Home at last," she said.

Lindsey's little sister Peggy tugged on my hand. She had lost her two front teeth since I last saw her, and her words came out in a whistle. "We want you to see your house."

Grandma took my other hand. "Everyone's been helping."

Only then did I notice the front porch. It had a fresh coat of white paint, and the sagging bits were standing straighter. "Daddy got the neighbors to help," Peggy said.

Grandma's step seemed lighter, and she giggled. "I missed you so much, I dreamed about you one day," she said. "Your mother, too. When I woke up, I realized I'd let the house overflow with stuff."

I stepped in the doorway and breathed in the smell of lemon. I'd never seen the floor shine like this, and the opening to the library glowed with light. I peeked into the room—the piles of newspapers were gone! Grandma hugged herself, a smile spreading across her face. "Miss Charlotte found a library that wanted to archive those old newspapers. And Lindsey's mother arranged for a thrift store to pick up the other stuff. Come and see."

In the kitchen the counters were bare except for bags of hotdog buns and relish trays for the cook-out.

"I don't understand," I said.

"Don't worry, we didn't touch your room," she said. "But when I woke up that day, I felt like all my life before was a sort of dream, and I needed to be up and doing."

Her face crumpled. "I did the right thing, didn't I?"

"Of course, Grandma. This is terrific!"

She pulled me into the living room, where a sofa and two chairs sat by the fireplace. "And look, we found these pictures of Franny and Dan." On the mantle was a series of frames with my parents in every one of them. "That's their honeymoon in Paris," Grandma said. She pointed to another one. "And this was when you were born."

My mother held a pink bundle in her arms, and her eyes looked out from the frame full of happiness, and something else. Hope.

ABOUT THE AUTHOR

Joyce McPherson is the author of books for young people as well as a director for Shakespearean theatre. She is also the mother of nine children, who give useful advice for her stories. She has never been to Camp Hawthorne, but still hopes for an invitation someday.

ACKNOWLEDGMENTS

Thank you to the moon and back to all the teachers, librarians, and bookstore wonders who have placed a copy of this book into the hands of a young person. And to all the bloggers who have spread the word, and to all the fans who have shared your enthusiasm with me and others, THANK YOU! I would thank you all by name if I could!

A special thank you to Garth, Heather, Alexie, Duncan, Andrew, David M., Grace, Connor, Luke, Emily, Laurie, Sally, Cathy, Marilyn, Laura, Kashmira, David Y., Meg, Tanya W., Jonathan, Elena, Kat, Lauren, Alexis, Catherine, Rachael, Lindsey, Mira, Jenn, Mary, Maria Luisa, Jenifer, Taylor, Kathleen, Jason, Wren, Von, Verne, Alejandro, Billy, Priscilla, Jessica, Louise, Tanya C., Andy, Michelle, Towana, Kim, Charles, Jane, Mette, Amanda, Ann, Andrea, Margaret, Debbie, Beth, Carolyn, Rich, Andrew, Alexandra, Eileen, Jess, Lisa, Gail, Mat, Connie, Lois and many others who read, listened and cheered this book to completion.